AFTER HIS FATHER IS MURDERED, DENNY McCUNE LIVES FOR ONE THING—REVENGE!

When he is just a boy, Denny sees his Pa killed by a gang of vicious men. He vows he will get revenge, and he does. One by one he guns the killers down.

Denny is acquitted by the court and moves on to another town, hoping to start a new life. But his reputation gets there first.

Known everywhere as a killer, Denny is trapped in a bitter range war as he helps his cousins defend their ranch. Forced to kill or be killed, Denny wonders how long he can survive as a gunfighter.

THE SAGA OF DENNY McCUNE

Budd and Burt Arthur

PAPERBACK LIBRARY, Inc.

New York

PAPERBACK LIBRARY EDITION
First Printing: June, 1968

*Paperback Library books are published by Paperback Library, Inc.
Its trademark, consisting of the words "Paperback Library" ac-
companied by an open book, is registered in the United States
Patent Office.* Paperback Library, Inc., 315 Park Avenue South,
New York, N.Y. 10010.

ONE

Denny McCune was only sixteen when he became a man. His maturity was due to circumstances over which, it was agreed by some of his elders, notably old Judge Phineas Hawks and Sheriff Buck Flowers, a boy of his age could not legally or logically be expected to have had any control. The slaying of his father, Jerry McCune, before his very eyes had so outraged him that it blinded him to all considerations, including respect for the law. So the fact that this gawky and shabbily dressed boy with a shapeless, floppy hat riding atop his mussed and overly long red hair, with his father's gunbelt buckled on around his narrow, hipless body and an old buffalo gun cradled in his arms had sought out the killers and had proceeded to exact a full measure of vengeance from each, was held to have been justified by the law.

However, there were those who refused to be silenced by the law and who insisted upon voicing their opinions. It was bad enough, they said, when a fully grown man took the law into his own hands; when a mere boy did it, it meant that he was born with the killer instinct in him, and they insisted that he should have been put away instead of being turned loose upon society. The guardians of the law ignored them and freed Denny. Despite that, the killing of three fully grown men by a mere boy continued to be the principal topic of conversation among the townspeople. The fact that there had been no witnesses to any of the killings did not matter. What did matter was the result, three dead bodies, and a boy who made no bones about having done the shooting.

Had there been any witnesses, they would have begun their version of what had happened with a description of the day. It was a warm, drowsy mid-afternoon in late August. The single street that was the town proper of Walkersville, Oklahoma, was bathed in bright sunshine and completely deserted. There was no activity of any kind, and there would be none till late afternoon when the wilting warmth of the day had tapered off. Then the witnesses would have launched into a recital of what they had heard and seen. It began when a big, bulky, pigeon-toed man who lumbered like a bear when he walked, sauntered out of Paddy Fogarty's saloon. He was Cuddy Lamson, the eldest of three brothers whose property and the McCunes' were separated by a stream whose ownership was still to be decided by the county court. He idled for a moment on the planked walk in front of the saloon, then moved to the low wooden curb. Just as he was about to step down into the rutted gutter, someone called his name and he stopped and turned his head. He stared a little when he saw Denny McCune with a half-raised buffalo gun in his dirty hands, standing some fifteen feet away. The boy had just stepped out of the shadowy depths of a vacant store's doorway.

"Reckon you know why I'm here," Cuddy heard Denny say evenly. "Only I'm gonna give you a better break than you gave my Pa. I'm gonna give you a chance to go for your gun before I cut down on you. Make your move."

"You . . . you crazy or something?" Cuddy sputtered, his round, heavily jowled face reddening. "The heat got you?"

"I'm waitin' on you."

"I don't draw on snotty-nosed kids," Cuddy retorted, trying to brazen his way out of a situation that he knew could turn out disastrously for him, unless he could overawe the boy holding his gun on him and cow him into backing down. "G'wan now. Get outta here before I get good an' sore and tan your backside for you."

The buffalo gun came up the barest bit higher and steadied again with the gaping, yawning muzzle holding on a line with the third button on Cuddy's sweat-wet denim shirt. He gulped and swallowed hard, painfully, judging by the wince that crossed his red face. Slowly he moved back from the curb. He stole a look at the saloon doorway, then he looked at Denny, apparently trying to figure his chances of reaching the safety of the doorway before the menacing buffalo gun could cut down on him. When he appeared to be satisfied that he could negotiate the distance safely with a giant leap that he was sure would take the boy by surprise, a thin trace of a scornful smile wrinkled the corners of his mouth. He was motionless for a moment, preparing himself for what he was about to do, then with a sudden

6

heave he flung himself around and leaped for the doorway. The buffalo gun thundered with the deep-throated booming of a cannon. The slug caught Cuddy while he was still in mid-air and tore his chest apart. He was dead even before he crashed on the walk about midway between the curb and the doorway. Quickly reloading, Denny melted back out of sight and waited. A white-aproned man, a storekeeper, appeared in front of his establishment far up the street and, hand-shading his eyes, peered downstreet. It was difficult to tell if he spotted the bulky, hunched-over body of Cuddy Lamson lying on the walk; apparently he didn't because he turned shortly and trudged back into his store.

Presently there was movement, cautious and unhurried movement inside Fogarty's doorway. A man poked his head out. He was Stevie Lamson, Cuddy's younger brother. He stared hard at the body on the walk, finally lifted his eyes and ranged a sweeping look across the street. He seemed to be surprised when he failed to see anyone about. He waited a moment or two though, before he stepped outside. Carefully avoiding Cuddy's outflung hand and a steadily widening pool of blood that was seeping out of the dead man, he emerged with his hand on his gun, shot a look up the street, then, turning his head, he looked downstreet. Slowly his hand came away from his gun. Suddenly he saw Denny standing on the walk, again with the buffalo gun half-raised. His eyes gleamed and his lips tightened.

"Oh!" he said. "Where'd you come from?" When Denny did not answer, Stevie asked: "You do this?" and he jerked his head at Cuddy's body.

"Uh-huh," Denny replied. "Only I gave him a chance to go for his gun before I cut down on him."

"You lousy young bastid," Stevie said thickly. "I'll fix you good."

His right hand dropped and clawed for his gun. His Colt was hardly more than halfway out of his holster when the buffalo gun roared again with its awing, deafening thunder. The slug tore into Stevie's body and spun him around and sent him careening blindly across the walk, his legs buckling under him. He stumbled and tripped over his own feet and fell across Cuddy's legs. Again Denny backed into

7

his shadowy refuge, quickly reloaded, and waited. He did not have to wait very long though, probably no more than a minute or so. The youngest of the Lamsons, twenty-year-old Robbie, whose youth scorned the use of patience and caution, came bounding out of the saloon with his gun in his hand. He hurdled his brothers' bodies, barely managed to avoid stepping into the pool that Stevie's blood was adding to, and skidded to a stop on the walk just a couple of strides short of the curb. Crouching a little belatedly, his eyes probed the buildings and the alleys across the street, seeking a sign of the man who had gunned down his brothers, ready to snap a shot at him the moment he spotted him. When he failed to spot anyone, he looked surprised, just as Stevie had. He relaxed, straightened up, and lowering his gun so that it hung at his side, looked up the street, again as Stevie had done before him. When he turned to look downstreet and saw Denny standing just a short distance away with the buffalo gun holding on him, he stared at the boy and finally said:

"So it's you, huh? Funny thing, you scurvy sonuvabitch, but after we got your old man, I wanted to go find you and kill you too. I don't like leaving things half done. Cuddy and Stevie talked me out've it. They said we didn't have anything to worry about from a snot-nose like you. I wish to hell I hadn'ta listened to them. They'd be alive now and you wouldn't."

As though his words had fallen on deaf ears, Denny told him quite simply:

"I was gonna give you the same chance I gave them. But being that you've got your gun in your hand, I won't have to. Soon's I think you're fixin' to shoot, I'm gonna cut down on you. I'm ready if you are. Go ahead and make your move."

Robbie needed no urging. His right arm jerked, his gun came sweeping up and he fired from the hip. He missed. But Denny didn't. The slug from the buffalo gun struck Robbie squarely and solidly. It spun him around drunkenly. He dropped his gun and tottered. He stumbled across the few reamining planks to the curb, swayed over it, and finally pitched out from it and fell headlong into the gutter, causing the dust to boil up around him briefly. After a moment it settled again. Now there was a rush of booted feet as Fogarty and a dozen or so men who had been lined up at his bar came dashing out. Townsmen and a couple of aproned shopkeepers came running from every direction, all of them converging upon the area of the saloon. Some of them thronged the walk with Fogarty and his customers while the others formed an uneven circle around Robbie Lamson's body. When a buckboard appeared at the head of the street and came wheeling into town all heads turned and all eyes focused on it and held on it as it came down the street.

"There's Buck now," somebody said.

"Yeah," somebody else added. "Ain't that the judge with him?"

"Uh-huh," a third man said.

When the sheriff, who was doing the driving, saw the crowd that had gathered around the saloon, he lashed his horse with the loose end of the reins, and the animal responded with a burst of speed. Flowers pulled up in the very middle of the street, dropped the reins in the judge's lap, jumped down from the buckboard and pushed through the onlookers to the side of Robbie Lamson and bent over him. When he came erect again, he was grim-faced and tight-lipped. He stepped up on the walk. The crowd gave way before him. He stopped in his tracks and stared hard when he saw the two older Lamsons. Apparently the way they lay on the walk and the sight of their blood that continued to seep out of them and run off and fill the cracks between the planks satisfied him that they too were dead.

"All right," he said authoritatively. "Who did it?"

When all heads turned again and everyone looked at Denny who stood motionlessly with the death-dealing buffalo gun still gripped in his hands, Flowers eyed him.

"You're Jerry McCune's boy, aren't you?" he asked.

"Yes, sir," Denny replied.

"You've growed some since I saw you last." When there was no response from Denny, Flowers asked: "You do this, boy? You kill these three?"

"Yes, sir."

"You mind telling me why?"

"They, the three o' th'm, killed my Pa."

"Oh? When was that?"

"This morning. Just before noon."

9

"You see th'm do it?"

"No, sir. I heard the shooting. When I looked outta the hay loft, I saw the three o' th'm ridin' away. So I knew they were the ones who did it."

Judge Hawks made his way to the sheriff's side and whispered something to him; Flowers nodded and said:

"Think we'd better do the rest of our talkin' in my office, boy. C'mon."

When he beckoned, Denny came trudging over to him; when he held out his hand for the buffalo gun, Denny surrendered it to him without a sign or a word of protest.

"Somebody go tell Lem Cantwell he's got three customers waitin' for him here," Flowers said, "and to come an' get th'm."

When Flowers gestured, the onlookers opened a path for him. With the sheriff on one side of him and the judge on the other, Denny, staring back stonily at those who looked at him, was escorted across the street and into the lawman's cubicle of an office. Many of the townspeople followed the three. When they gathered on the walk outside of Flowers' office and pressed too close to the window, he closed the door and yanked down the threadbare shade over the window, shutting out the sun as well as the curious. Then as he backed against the door, he propped up the buffalo gun against the wall nearest him, and said: "Sit down, Judge." He waited till Hawks made his way around the desk, the only piece of furniture in the office aside from the armchair behind it and a straightbacked and uninviting chair that stood in a far corner. When the judge eased himself down into the armchair, Flowers turned to Denny and said: "All right, boy. Supposin' you tell us everything that happened."

Denny nodded and said: "Yes, sir." Suddenly he snatched off his hat and holding it in his grimy hand began with: "Pa an' me'd been up in the hills for a couple o' days huntin' an' trappin'."

Denny continued. "When we got back this morning, Pa took the horses down to the stream to water th'm while I climbed up to the loft to get some hay and feed for the stalls." He wiped his nose and mouth with the back of his hand. "Couple o' times I kinda peeked out. I could see Pa and the horses real plain. Pa was standing up a ways from

10

the bank watchin' the horses drink their fill. All uva sudden I heard some shooting. I took a quick look out. Pa was layin' on the ground on his face. I saw the Lamsons on their side o' the stream and they were ridin' up the bank. That's how I knew it was them who killed Pa. Guess that's about all there is to tell. 'Cept that by the time I got down to where Pa was layin', he was dead and they were gone."

There was no comment from Flowers. He took his gaze from Denny and looked at the judge, apparently expecting and waiting for him to do whatever questioning was to be done. Hawks wore a deepening frown on his face. He leaned a little forward over the desk, then hunching over it on his folded arms, looked up at Denny.

"How old are you, boy?" he asked.

"Sixteen."

"Didn't it occur to you, son, to notify the sheriff as quickly as you could so that he could apprehend . . . that is, bring in your father's slayers and bring them up for trial, instead of taking the law into your own hands? Or don't you have any faith in the law?"

"Oh, I've got faith in it, sure," the boy answered quickly. "Pa used to say that the law's a good thing and that everybody oughta look up to it."

"Still you ignored the law and . . . "

"Excuse me, Judge," the boy said, interrupting Hawks. "But all I could think of was that Pa was dead, that the Lamsons had killed him, and being that I was the only one left, that it was up to me to do something to get hunk with th'm. And that's what I did. Way I see it now, I saved the law the trouble of goin' after the Lamsons and having to bring th'm in and then puttin' th'm on trial. They'da swung for what they done . . . did to Pa. So what's the difference b'tween what the law woulda done to th'm and what I did to th'm?

The judge stared at him. Then he eased back in the armchair. He looked long and hard at the boy, who met his eyes unwaveringly. When he beckoned, the sheriff came striding across the office to the desk and bent over it, and standing backturned to Denny, conferred in whispered tones with Hawks. After a minute or so, Flowers straightened up and turned around and sauntered back to

11

the door and resumed his post there. The judge cleared his throat.

"Son," he began, and Denny looked at him. "What you did was wrong. You had no right to take the law into your own hands. If everyone did that, there wouldn't be any need for the law. Can you understand that?"

"Yes, sir."

"Have you any relatives around here? Any who would take you in and give you a home?"

"Not around here. In Texas. And that's where I'm aimin' to go when you say it's all right for me to go."

"Where in Texas?" Flowers asked, and Denny turned his head in the sheriff's direction.

"Place called Ludlow," the boy replied. "Pa's kinfolk, the McEntees, live there. Pa always said that if anything ever happened to him before I was full growed, I should go to them, and they would take me in."

"Wait a minute," Flowers commanded. He strode back to the desk and picked up a folded-over newspaper that had been pushed aside almost to the very edge, unfolded it, and looking around at Denny, said: "Wait'll you hear this, boy. Maybe you'll change your mind about goin' to Texas." He ran his eye over the front page, stopped his searching when he came to the item that he was seeking, and pointing to it with a thick, broken-nailed finger, read aloud:

TEXAS RANGE WAR SPREADING

• • •

A bitter range war, the worst that Texas has ever known, that has already claimed eleven lives and the loss of thousand of dollars worth of property and cattle, is reported to be spreading with alarming rapidity. Authorities in Ludlow County where violence has flared to uncontrollable heights admit their inability to cope with it.

Ludlow's Sheriff Dave Smith has sent an urgent appeal to Governor Stanton Wheeler for help. But it does not appear likely that help will be forthcoming very soon.

Flowers folded the paper and put it down again, turned to Denny, and asked:

"Well, boy? Still think you wanna go to Texas?"

"Yes, sir," was the quietly spoken reply.

The sheriff, unable to conceal his surprise, stared at him unbelievingly.

Flowers jerked around to the Judge Hawks, threw up his hands, and said disgustedly:

"I give up, Judge. He's too much for me. He's all yours."

"Thanks," Hawks said dryly. He leveled a long look at Denny. "I don't understand you, boy. But if the prospect of walking into the bitterest range war that Texas has ever known doesn't deter you, nothing that I can say will impress you. Give him his gun, Sheriff, and let him go."

When Denny clapped his hat on his head and started forward, Flowers reached for the buffalo gun, handed it to him and stepped aside. Denny opened the door, nodded over his shoulder and went out. The people who were still standing outside of Flowers' office looked at the boy as he stepped out on the walk. As before, he stared back stonily at them. As he started down the street, apparently to get his horse, a plain-faced, somberly dressed woman and a pretty girl called to him, and he stopped and looked around and waited till they came up to him. They were the Dawkinses, neighbors of the McCunes. Lovey, the Dawkinses' fifteen-year-old daughter, was their only child and their pride and joy. She had long nurtured a fondness for the boy.

"We want you to know how terribly sorry we are, Denny," Mrs. Dawkins began. "Both Lovey and I were stunned when we heard about your father." She paused for a brief moment, then she continued with: "Denny, you and Lovey have always gotten along so nicely, wouldn't you like to come and live with us? We have a big house as you know and plenty of room, and . . . "

"I'm obliged to you, ma'am," Denny said, interrupting her, "for offering to take me in. But I've got some kin living down in Texas, and being that Pa wanted me to go to them if anything happened to him, that's where I'll be going."

Lovey looked disappointed. Noticing it, he said quickly: "Now don't take on so. I won't be so far away, no

13

more'n three or four days' ride from here, so I'll be able to come an' visit with you every now an' then." Then to Mrs. Dawkins, he said: "Like I said, ma'am, I'm obliged to you."

Lifting his hat to the women, he turned on his heel and marched off down the street.

TWO

Denny was so confident that he would not be held for the vengeance killing of his father's slayers, and that his youth would win his freedom for him, that his saddlebags were already packed to capacity with foodstuffs for the long haul to Texas. He had cleaned out the cupboard at home of everything that it had held. As soon as he returned from the sheriff's office, he began the long ride to Ludlow.

Now it was three days since he had left Walkersville. He was trying to decide what he would have for his midday meal, an hour or so from then, when his keen ears picked up the distant beat of a horse's hoofs. Tightening his grip on the buffalo gun that he hand-held across the saddle, he slowed his mount to a trot while he scanned the sun-swept prairie for a sign of the horseman. Presently a mounted man heading in a northeastward direction came into view. When he spotted Denny, he swung around and came drumming toward him at a swift lope. In a matter of minutes he came up to Denny in a flurry of hoofbeats and reined in in front of him. Pulling up too, Denny ran an appraising eye over the stranger. He was a rather seedy-looking individual with quick, darting eyes set in a thin, weak-chinned face that bore a week's growth of beard on it. Easing himself in the saddle, he said with a sly little grin that parted his lips and revealed yellowish teeth:

"Lookin' at you, boy, reminds me of the time I ran away from home. That what you're doing?"

"Nope," Denny replied. "Got nothing an' nobody to run away from."

"Oh?" the man said. He looked interestedly at the boy's horse. "That's a good lookin' horse you've got under you."

"He's a heap better'n just good lookin'."

There was no response from the stranger. He swung

14

down from his own horse, and hitching up his sagging gun-belt, took a step toward Denny when the buffalo gun leveled and the hammer was pulled back. "That's close enough," Denny told him. "You come 'ny closer, I'll blow you outta your boots."

The man stopped dead in his tracks and stared at the boy.

"Now, careful-like with your left hand," Denny commanded, "unbuckle your gunbelt and let it fall."

The fire-blackened muzzle of the buffalo gun yawned and gaped hungrily at the surprised stranger.

"What . . . what's the idea?" he demanded blusteringly.

"This old gun o' mine makes an awfully big hole in a man when I point it at him and pull the trigger," Denny said.

The man frowned. But he obeyed, unbuckled his gunbelt with his left hand, and let it drop at his feet.

"Now turn yourself around," Denny ordered. Again the man obeyed. In an instant Denny was off his horse; in another instant or two he was back on him with the captured gunbelt buckled and hanging from his thin left wrist and the buffalo gun again holding on the backturned man. "Get up on your horse and start riding," the latter was instructed.

The frustrated man hoisted himself up on his horse.

"Hell of a thing to do to a man," he complained. "To leave him out here without a gun when there's no telling who or what he's liable to run into."

"I know, and it's a shame," Denny agreed. "Specially when there's always a chance o' his runnin' into somebody who's on the dodge and tryin' to give the law the slip and who's got an eye out for a better an' faster horse than his own. Sorry to disappoint you, mister. But I aim to keep my horse for myself. Now if you don't want that posse that's after you to ketch up with you, you'd better start riding."

The man glared at him. He opened his mouth to say something. But the muzzle of the old gun awed him. Clamping his jaws shut and downing the rush of angry words that had come surging up to his lips, he flashed an angry, over-the-shoulder look at the boy, and rode away. Denny followed him with his eyes till he disappeared in the distance. Then he too wheeled and loped off.

15

It was on the morning of the fifth day that he rode into Ludlow and halted at the entrance to the town and ranged his eyes over it. An unusually long and somewhat crookedly laid-out street spread away before him. All of the stores, and that included two saloons, were shuttered and tightly locked, save for a single store about midway down the street, whose windows were shuttered but whose door stood wide open. In front of it and drawn up at the curb was a farm wagon. Three saddled horses that stood quietly side-by-side were tied to a rear wheel. Two rifle-armed horsemen who kept wheeling about seemed to be watching the far corners. They half-raised their rifles when Denny came riding down the street, and one of them yelled something that he couldn't make out. He sensed that it wasn't meant for him when there was almost immediate reaction to the man's cry. Four other men, with obviously hastily snatched up rifles in their hands, spilled out of the store and onto the walk and looked hard at the oncoming youthful rider. One of them, a huge redheaded man who towered over the others on the walk, motioned to them to stay where they were, and crossed it to the curb and halted there and gave Denny a head-tilted look, suddenly laughed and said to him:

"You're the spittin' image of your old man, boy. What's he name you?"

"Denny."

"Uh-huh. For his old man. Know who I am?"

"Yes, sir. The McEntee, Pa used to call you. Other time he spoke of you as Big Matt."

The redheaded man grinned broadly, stepped down into the gutter, and halting at Denny's side, thrust up his big right hand to the boy. Gravely Denny shook hands with him.

"How come Jerry didn't come with you?" the man asked.

"B'cause he's dead."

Matt stared hard at him.

"Dead?" he repeated. "Y'mean some no-good so-an'-so killed him?"

Just as he had told the story of his father's slaying to the sheriff and to the judge, Denny related it to his father's kinsman. Matt listened to it attentively—as did the others,

16

who couldn't help but hear it, in view of their nearness—and without interruption, and without once taking his eyes from the boy's earnest young face. When Denny finished his recital, Matt commented:

"You were awf'lly lucky to get off that easy. Another judge mighta held you for trial and you coulda wound up in prison. How old did you say you are?"

"Sixteen. Be seventeen next May."

"And you took on those three Lamson men one after another just like that?"

Meeting his eyes, Denny answered simply:

"Guess I went through with what I had t'do because there wasn't anybody else around t'do it for me."

Big Matt eyed him obliquely and said as he turned to re-enter the store:

"Stay put here, Denny, while we get loaded up. Then we'll head for home."

He trudged back into the store and the other men who had come out followed him inside. Moments later they began to load the wagon with flour, coffee and sugar, and followed them with many smaller things. One of the mounted men, a redheaded youth of about nineteen or twenty, brought his horse up alongside of Denny's, grinned at him and said:

"I'm Matt McEntee too. And that," he added, half-turning and indicating the other horsemen with a nod: "That's my brother, Pat."

When Denny looked at him, Pat, who appeared to be a bit younger than his brother, and was dark-haired instead of redheaded, gave him a half-salute and said to him:

"Hi, Denny. Glad to have you with us."

"Thanks," Denny responded.

The boys' father poked his head out of the store.

"Save the gab for later on," he called out curtly. "For when we're home. Right now you've got something a heap more important to do. Keep lookin' around like I told you to do. I don't want Green's outfit or that damned Horton and his crew slippin' into town and jumpin' us."

"Right, Pop," Pat answered.

His father withdrew his head.

"You c'n start earning your keep right now, Denny," Pat said. "Keep watchin' the alleys around us. 'Course if you

17

see anything that doesn't look just right to you, holler, and we'll come a-hustling."

Young Matt had been eying the buffalo gun.

"Haven't seen one o' those Sharps 30-30s since I was, we-ll, about ten or maybe twelve," he said. "Pop had one o' th'm."

"This isn't a Sharps," Denny said, interrupting him. "It's an old buffalo gun."

"Oh? That Sharps sounded like a cannon when it went off. And if had a kick to it like a mule."

Then Pat turned to his brother and said: "Matt, suppose we both ride off a ways, huh? You go up the street while I go down a piece and kinda take a look-see."

"Sure," Matt said, pulled away from Denny and jogged up the street, while Pat wheeled his horse and trotted him away in the opposite direction.

Turning and watching Matt first, then Pat, Denny saw each range his gaze over both sides of the street. When he heard bootheels thump on the planked walk, he turned his head and saw Big Matt come out to the wagon with a slab of bacon riding atop his right shoulder. Satisfied, Denny turned his gaze the other way. His attention was attracted by something that gleamed metallically in a narrow alley directly across the street.

"Look out!" he yelled, raised the buffalo gun and fired.

It exploded with a deafening roar. The McEntee boys came pounding back and pulled their snorting horses to a sliding stop at Denny's side and asked as one:

"What was it? Y'see somebody?"

"In that alley over there!" he gasped, pointing to it. "There was a man in there kinda bending over. I saw him just as he was standing up and raisin' his rifle. I hollered and took a shot at him. I musta hit him before he could shoot. He went over backwards."

Again men with rifles in their hands poured out of the store and on to the walk. It was McEntee himself, gun in hand, who waved his men back and ordered Denny and his sons to stay where they were while he investigated. They saw him mount the opposite walk, saw him sidle up to the alley and steal a guarded, cautious look inside, then straighten up and move into the alley, stand motionlessly for a moment and then bend over something. Minutes later,

18

with his gun shoved down in his holster, he emerged from the alley, crossed the walk and stepped down into the gutter. The boys leveled questioning eyes at him. But they held their tongues and waited for him to answer their unasked questions. Raising his eyes to Denny, he said:

"Thanks, boy. That's one I owe you." To his sons, he said: "Marv Horton. He's been gunning for me ever since that night he an' his brother Vic and their crew tried to raid our place and burn us out. We got Vic, and Marv woulda got me just now if it hadn't been for Denny."

"That gun o' yours makes an even louder blast than that Sharps I was telling you about," young Matt said to Denny.

"And it does one helluva job on a man," Big Matt added grimly. "Specially from up close like from here to that alley. That slug you pegged into Marv just abut tore the front o' him wide open. Bloodiest mess I ever saw. Pat, wanna go see if Dave Smith is in his office? Like him to know about this from us and while we're still here instead o' leaving it to him or somebody else to find Marv and wonder what happened to him."

Pat didn't answer. Apparently his father did not expect him to. He wheeled his horse and loped down the street. Following him with their eyes, the others saw him pull up near the corner, dismount and drop the reins at his horse's feet, hitch up his levis as he mounted the walk and cross it to a closed door over which hung a faded sign. When McEntee saw Denny crane his neck in an effort to make out what it said, he grunted and said simply:

"Sheriff."

"Oh!" Denny said.

Pat knocked on the door. When there was no response, they saw him try the doorknob. Just as he was about to knock a second time, the door was opened and they saw a man peered out at Pat. The two talked briefly. Then, as Pat stepped back, the man came out and closed the door behind him. As he started up the street, Pat returned to his horse, climbed up on him, wheeled him, and matching strides with the sheriff, came up the street with him. When they neared the alley, Pat swerved away to rejoin his brother and Denny while his father stepped up on the walk, nodded to the lawman and led him into the alley. The boys could hear their voices but not what was being said. When the two men finally emerged from the alley and halted on the walk in front of it, Denny saw the lawman peer hard at him. In turn Denny was able to get a good look at the man. He was middle-aged and pudgy rather than stocky, and baldheaded. The star that he wore pinned to his shirtpocket looked to be made of tin and was tarnished around the edges. He was unarmed, and that in itself made the boy wonder about him. Smith looked more like a shopkeeper to whom his apron tied around his middle felt more comfortable and certainly far more natural than a buckled-on gunbelt.

Presently the sheriff and Big Matt sauntered across the walk to the curb. Smith dug in his pants pocket, and after some tugging and yanking, succeeded in hauling out a pair of metal-rimmed spectacles, which he put on. Waving McEntee back, he stepped down into the gutter, moved around Pat and young Matt to Denny's side, looked up at him, and pushing his glasses higher up on his nose, asked curtly:

"What's your name?"

"Denny McCune."

"When'd you hit town?"

"Just a while ago. Oh, no more'n about half 'n hour ago."

"What made you pick on Ludlow instead o' some other place?"

"Lost my Pa, and being that I was left alone, I came here to live with Pa's kinfolk, the McEntees."

"And just happened to find th'm right here," Smith said dryly. "Almost like they were expecting you and waiting for you."

"That's right," Denny said evenly.

"How old are you?"

"Sixteen."

"You look older'n that to me," the sheriff said. "More like eighteen and maybe even nineteen." When Denny made no response, Smith, eying the holstered gun that was buckled on around the boy's waist, asked: "Know how to use that thing?"

"Yeah, sure."

"What've you got in those saddlebags, s'more guns?" Before Denny could answer, Smith opened one bag, peered

20

into it and hauled out the holstered gunbelt that Denny had taken from the man whom he had encountered on the prairie. "You travel around pretty well armed for a sixteen-year-old, don't you?"

"Got that gun from a man I ran into on the prairie," Denny said, and his expression indicated that he regretted having said it.

"Mean he gave it to you just like that?"

"Well, no. Y'see, this man looked like he was on the dodge. When he began makin' eyes at my horse, I knew what he was thinking. So I threw down on him quick, made him drop his gun and back off. I grabbed the gun and, still holding my own gun on him, made him get going. He beefed about bein' left without a gun. But he musta seen that I meant business and that he wasn't gonna get 'nywhere's with me tryin' to talk me into givin' him back his gun. I wasn't lookin' to have him trail me and jump me later on and take my horse and leave me his. I was gonna give the gun to Mr. McEntee when I met up with him. Anyway, that's how I got the gun. In case you're wondering about this one," and Denny pointed to the one he was wearing, "it was my Pa's."

"How come you didn't plug that feller right off?" Smith asked. "Then you wouldn'ta had anything to worry about from him."

"I don't go 'round pluggin' people 'less there's call for it."

"How'd you know Marv Horton was fixin' to shoot? Just because he had a rifle in his hands?"

"He was doing more'n that. He wasn't just holding it in his hands. He was aiming it at Mr. McEntee. That's why I cut down on him. Before he could shoot."

"I'm gonna ask you once more, young feller. I wanna know how old you are, and I want the truth outta you, y'hear?"

"Like I told you before, I'm sixteen."

"I think you're eighteen and maybe even nineteen. So that makes you old enough to stand trial. So I'm takin' you in."

"Like hell you are!" Big Matt yelled. In an instant he was in the gutter, and as the sheriff reached up to relieve Denny of the buffalo gun, the enraged McEntee brushed

21

him aside with a sweep of his brawny left arm and sent him stumbling away. "You fellers finished?" he yelled at the three men who had been loading the wagon. "If you are, let's get rolling!"

"All right, Mister McEntee," Smith said. His spectacles were hanging from one ear and there was a red blotch on his face where Big Matt's heavy hand had come in contact with it. "When the Rangers get here, you an' him will be the first ones they'll bring in. And if you wanna know what the charge'll be, I'll tell you. Him for murder and you for puttin' him up to it. You figured he'd get away with killing Marv Horton for you on account o' him not being old enough to be punished for doin' it." He eased his spectacles off his ear and put them on properly. However, the red blotch remained. "For now you're free to go. But when the Rangers get here . . . "

Seeing the door to the store close from the inside and one of his men climb up to the driver's seat and unwind the reins from around the pulled-back handbrake, McEntee shouldered Smith aside and strode over to the wagon and untied his horse. The remaining two men untied their horses too. The three climbed up into the saddle at the same time. The wagon pulled away from the curb. Big Matt and the two men with him loped away, overtook the wagon and rode in advance of it.

"Ler's go," young Matt said, and Pat and Denny wheeled around after him.

Quickly they caught up with the wagon and pulled into position behind it and followed it as it rumbled down the deserted street. Minutes later, when the little party reached the far end and took the open road that led to the McEntee place, which was some seven miles southwestward of Ludlow, Big Matt yelled something. Instantly the horses were given their heads and broke into a swift gallop.

THREE

The free-running horses, delighted at having been given their heads, devoured the miles that lay between Ludlow and the McEntee spread. Then with great suddenness, the three horsemen riding ahead of the wagon and the wagon

22

too slowed their killing pace and wheeled through a wooden archway at the top of which was a signboard that bore the McEntee brand, a boxed-off McE. Denny had already noticed the brand on the McEntee horses.

Following his cousins through the archway, he looked about him interestedly. About a hundred feet in from the road was a solidly built two-story house with a roofed-over veranda fronting it and running around both sides. Closer at hand though, and on the right, was a low, squat and rather drab looking building that he learned later on was the bunkhouse in which the McEntee hands were quartered. Just beyond it was the corral, a sizeable enclosure with trampled, scuffed-up dirt surfacing it. The corral was empty, a sign that the range war in which the McEntees had become involved did not exempt their horses from feeling the wrath of raiders. On the left and diagonally opposite the bunkhouse and the corral was the barn, a towering structure that dwarfed any that Denny had ever seen before. In fact, everything that he had seen that far of the McEntee place impressed him tremendously. The barn's door was closed. Despite it, he could hear quite plainly the McEntee horses' hoofs pawing on the barn's floorboards.

A rifle-armed man poked his head out of the hay loft and greeted the little party with a grin and a wave of his hand. The door was rolled back. Everyone dismounted. McEntee was the first to lead his horse up the ramp, then the others followed him. The wagon had braked to a stop in front of the barn; now it moved off, rumbled away toward the house, and rounding it, disappeared behind it.

Propping up the buffalo gun against a side wall in the huge and shadowy building, Denny proceeded to unsaddle his horse, glancing around at the others at the same time.

When Pat and young Matt started to lead their horses down an aisle between two long rows of stalls, the latter turned his head and called to Denny: "C'mon, Denny. Bring him down here." Leading his horse by the bridle, Denny followed the McEntee brothers. The stalls at the far end of the aisle were unoccupied. When Pat stopped and pointed and said: "In there, Denny," the boy nodded and guided his horse into the indicated stall, removed the bridle and hung it on a nail. "There's water and feed and salt in there, Denny," Pat called out to him. "So leave him be."

23

Big Matt and the two men who had ridden with him had already left the barn, Denny discovered when he followed his cousins to the door. Pat and Matt led him toward the house. As they neared it, he could see two small, fenced-in flower gardens, one on each side of the gravel path that led to the front door. Instead of going in the front way, the boys veered off and Denny followed them around the house to the rear.

With Pat leading the way, they entered the house. The biggest and roundest table that Denny had ever seen, with eight straightbacked chairs pushed in close to it, filled the middle of the over-sized kitchen. A red-checkered cloth covered the table. A stove that Denny was sure had to be the largest that he would ever see anywhere, and a wooden wall rack that held six rifles caught his eye as he followed the McEntee boys through the kitchen, out through a portiered doorway and up a flight of thinly carpeted stairs. A hall runner that ran the length of the upper floor cushioned their steps. Denny bumped into Pat when the latter stopped abruptly and pointed to the far end of the floor.

"The last door, Denny," he said. "That'll be your room. Oh, think I'd better warn you right off. Don't leave your clothes layin' around. Hang everything away. If you don't, our sister, Kate, who rides herd on us and that includes Pop, will give you no peace. She's the woman of the house and she runs it same's she does us and long's you live here, she'll boss you too. Where've you got your clothes, in your saddlebags?"

Denny shook his head.

"Nope," he replied. "They're on me."

"Oh?" Pat said. He ranged an appraising and critical eye over the boy, rubbed his chin thoughtfully with his right thumb and finally said: "We'll have to do something about that."

"Leave that to Kate," young Matt said. "She'll fix him up."

Someone came up the stairs, someone who was far lighter-footed than any of them. The three turned their heads and looked back. A girl with flaming red hair, who was even prettier than Lovey Dawkins and several years older, topped the stairs, stopped and looked in the boys' direction.

24

"There she is now," Pat announced. "Kate, this is our cousin, Denny McCune. You've heard Pop speak of his father, Jerry. You wanna say h'llo to Denny, don't you?"

"Yes, of course," Kate answered. She came down the landing quickly and gracefully, flashed Denny a warm, shiny-toothed smile and greeted him with: "Hello, Denny McCune. Nice to have you with us."

"We all owe Denny something," young Matt told her. "Marv Horton was all set to take a shot at Pop when Denny spotted him and blasted him before he could shoot."

Kate caught her breath.

"Kate, you wanna show Denny his room?" Pat asked. "He knows where it is because I just pointed it out to him."

The girl nodded and said:

"Come on, Denny."

The McEntees turned and went downstairs while Kate, stepping ahead of Denny, led him down the corridor, opened the door to the room that was to be his, and holding it wide, turned as he halted in the doorway and ranged his eyes around the room. He took in everything, from the curtained window to the bureau and the blanket-covered bed to the neat, thin-worn piece of carpet that covered most of the floor.

"I think you'll be quite comfortable in here," Kate said after a brief silence.

"It's nice," he told her, turning to her and meeting her steady green eyes. "Real nice."

She looked at the gunbelt that he was wearing, holding her gaze longest on the gunbutt that jutted out of the holster.

"Aren't you rather young to be wearing a gun?" she asked, her question as well as her critical expression reflecting her disapproval.

"Never used to wear one," he told her gravely. "It was my Pa's. When he was killed, I took it and put it on. I've been wearin' it ever since."

Surprise showed in her suddenly widened eyes.

"Your father's dead? I'm sorry to hear that, Denny. Does my father know?"

"Yeah, sure. Told him right off."

"When did it happen?"

He thought a moment, then he replied:

"Five days ago."

He propped up the buffalo gun against the bed, plopped his shapeless hat on top of it, unbuckled and took off the gunbelt, buckled it again and hung it from the nearest bedpost, and glanced at her.

"That's better," she said.

"You don't like guns, do you?"

Ignoring his question, she asked:

"How old are you, Denny?"

"Sixteen."

"I don't approve of guns in the hands of sixteen-year-old boys," she said bluntly.

"I know what you're thinking," she continued. "That if it hadn't been for you and the fact that you were armed, my father wouldn't be alive now. Don't think I've fogotten that or that I'm not grateful to you." Wisely he held his tongue. "I don't suppose it's any of my business when you come right down to it. So you do as you please. If you want to wear your father's gun and hang on to that other thing, that's your privilege. You aren't accountable to me for what you do."

"And I kinda think I oughta be long's I live here," he said.

She gave him an odd, head-tilted look. Then a little smile broke out over her face. "All right, Denny. We've disposed of the guns. Now we'll go on to other things. Have you any other clothes besides those that you're wearing?"

"Nope."

"I think we can remedy that for you," Kate said after a moment-long study of the boy. "Pat has some things that he's out-grown and that I had intended to get rid of some time ago. Good thing I never got around to doing it. I'll go through them and pick out what's still usable and what I think will fit you or can be made to fit you. Now about your hair. Didn't they have a barber where you come from?"

"Yeah, sure. Only trouble was that any time Pa an' me hit town, Mr. Cantwell, the barber, who happened to be the undertaker too, always seemed to be busy fixin' up somebody who'd just died so's he could be buried. So I never could make c'nnections with him to get my hair cut."

"You're shaggier than my dog was, and I used to think he was the shaggiest thing anywhere," Kate announced.

"Get that chair," she commanded, pointing to a hard, straightbacked chair that stood on the far side of the bed, "and bring it over to the window while I go get my scissors and a towel, . . . oh, yes, and a paper sack. When I finish with you, you're going to wash your hair, and just to make sure you do it right, I'll stand by and watch."

He eyed her a little obliquely then smiled resignedly.

"Mind if I ask you something?"

Her slender shoulders lifted in a shrug.

"Matt's the oldest. Where d'you come in, before Pat or after?"

She dimpled prettily, smiled and answered: "After. I'm the youngest, the baby of the family."

"About how young?"

"I'll be eighteen come Christmas."

"And I'll be seventeen come May. That makes you only one year older'n me."

"One and a half," she corrected him.

He gave the matter some frowning thought, and finally conceded: "Yeah, that's right."

"Of course it's right," she said rather loftily. "I'm very good at figures. My mother was a school teacher and she taught me well."

It was about an hour or two later when he came downstairs to the kitchen and found Pat and young Matt idling about while a backturned Chinaman busied himself at the stove. The McEntee brothers looked up, stared a little at Denny, looked at each other and exchanged winks.

"You run into some Injuns on the warpath, friend?" Matt asked him, peering at the boy's head. "You must've, because you sure look like you've been scalped."

Denny grinned again and said:

"You'll have to figger that one out for yourself. All I'm gonna tell you is that Kate sent me down here to have you fellers take a look at me an' see what kind of a job she did on me. She cut my hair and fixed me up in your clothes, Pat, and she dug up a pair o' your old boots, Matt, because mine were just about worn through. What do I tell her? I look all right to you?"

The McEntee brothers came forward for a closer look at him.

"You look fine, Denny," Pat told him.

27

"Talk about clothes makin' the man," Matt said. "You're a doggoned good lookin' young feller."

"Hey, Ming," Pat called to the Chinaman. "Turn around and say hello to our young cousin, Denny McCune."

Ming, stubby, about half as round as he was tall, and full-faced, turned himself around, gave Denny a broad, toothy smile, bowed and said:

"Hallo, Cousin McClune. You one fine young feller."

"Well, now that that's over with," Pat said. "I'm hungry. How about it, Ming?"

"Soon," the Chinaman said over his shoulder. "Fixing now."

"We're going to spell some o' the men who've been guarding our stock," Matt said to Denny. "So's they can ride in and get themselves some grub too. Wanna trail along with us, or d'you wanna stay put?"

"I'm going with you," Denny answered.

"You don't have to, y'know," Pat said.

"I wanna do whatever I can," Denny said. "Wanna earn my keep. I'm not used to sittin' around. When Pa was alive, I had my chores to do same's he had his. So I don't see 'ny reason why I shouldn't do things around here too."

Matt shrugged and said:

"Whatever you say, Denny. None of us is used to layin' around either. Even though we've got a crew of ten men to work the place—good, experienced hands they are too— we pitch in and lend a hand wherever we can."

"And nobody's ever told us to," Pat added.

Neither Kate nor her father joined them when Ming served them their midday meal. When they finished, the three pushed back from the table and got up. When Pat and Matt pushed their chairs close in to the table, Denny did the same with his. When the two older youths trooped upstairs to get their hats and rifles, Denny followed them. Kate, with her arms filled with soiled bed linen, was coming down the landing when they topped the stairs.

"Well?" she demanded of Denny, halting squarely in front of him.

Matt answered for him.

"You did a fine job on him, Kate," he told his sister.

"That's right, Sis," Pat added. "Swell job. Only I don't think we oughta let him show his face in town. If we do,

28

Matt and I won't stand a chance with any o' the girls. They won't be able to see us for dust and it'll be on account o' him."

"Come on, Matt. Time's a-wasting," Pat said. "We'd better get a move on if we're gonna go spell some o' the crew."

"Right," Matt responded, hitching up his belt. He strode off after his brother. He was within a couple of strides of his room when he turned his head and called out over his shoulder: "Meet us out front, Denny, or down at the barn."

Kate leveled an apprehensive, frowning look at the boy.

"I'm not so sure that you should be going with them," she said. "There's liable to be trouble and that means shooting, and I don't like the idea of you getting caught in it. Couple of times now the raiders have jumped our crew and run off some of our stock. And a couple of our men have been shot."

"Oh, I'll be all right," he answered, stepped around her and started down the landing to his room.

Half-turning around, she followed him with her eyes. Suddenly though, she marched after him. He had just entered his room and moved toward the bed to pick up his hat that he had left lying there with the buffalo gun propped up close by. The old, battered and shapeless hat was gone, and in its place was a far better one. He picked it up when he was suddenly aware of someone standing in the open doorway and watching him. As he looked doorward, Kate said:

"It should fit you. Try it on."

He clapped it on his head. She stepped inside and dumped the bedclothes on the bed, came up to him and tugged at the brim of the hat, bringing it down a bit more in the front. Then she glided back from him, nodded and said: "That's better."

They heard her brothers go down the stairs.

"I want to tell you something," she began in a low voice. "You don't know the girls around here. I do and I don't like them. They're too forward. I don't ever want to hear of you getting mixed up with any of them, or even making eyes at any of them. They aren't your kind. They aren't

29

good enough for you."

"I don't think you'll ever have to worry about that."

"I hope not."

"If I have to make eyes at anyone, be all right if I make eyes at you?"

Their eyes met and held. It was Kate who finally averted hers, blushing under his steady gaze.

"You're the prettiest girl I've ever seen. So why should I wanna go and look at somebody else?"

She kissed him so suddenly, taking him completely by surprise so that he was unprepared for it, and a little startled. Instinctively he brought up his hands and reached for her. She pushed them off, and backed away from him, her face a deep crimson, and told him:

"You'd better go. The boys will be wondering what's taking you so long."

He caught up the buffalo gun and started out, stopped outside the room and looked back at her.

"Go on," she said with a gesture.

He turned and headed for the stairs.

"Be careful, Denny," she called after him as he reached the stairs and went down. "If there's any trouble, don't get mixed up in it."

He didn't answer. He pushed through the portiered doorway and rounded the oversized table without a word to Ming, who was again busy at the stove and who looked to him and flashed a wide-mouthed smile as Denny hurried out the back door.

FOUR

Young Matt and Pat McEntee, mounted and with the butts of their rifles jutting out of their saddleboots, were waiting impatiently for Denny in front of the barn when he came racing down from the house clutching the buffalo gun. As he came panting over to them he spied his own horse, saddled and ready for him, idling beyond them.

"What took you so long?" Matt wanted to know.

"Got talkin' with Kate," Denny heaved at him as he hauled himself up on his horse, "and one thing kinda led to another."

"Uh-huh. Always does with Kate," Pat said with a grin. "Let's go." As they loped off from the barn and cut squarely between the bunkhouse and the corral, Pat, who was riding on Denny's right, said to him: "I know what talkin' to Kate means. Either you wind up in a hassle with her because woman-like she sees things different than a man does, or you suddenly realize you've chucked away a whole hour jawin' away with her about nothing in particular."

"She's gotta talk to somebody," Matt, who rode on Denny's left, said. Then Matt whacked his mount on the rump with the flat of his right hand. It was an explosive slap that carried little or no sting or pain to it, and sounded a lot worse than it was because his startled horse snorted protestingly, creating the impression that he had been hit hard. The horse bounded away with Matt, forcing the other two to quicken their pace in order to overtake him. They ranged up alongside of him after a brief but spirited run and galloped along with him. The land over which they were riding was level and thickly carpeted with rich green, lush grass that was ideal for grazing. It spread away on every side about as far as the eye could see. Denny twisted around once and looked back. There was no sign of the house. But he glimpsed the towering barn even though that too was rapidly fading from sight. Squaring around again, he turned to Pat and asked:

"How big's the McE?"

"Oh, about forty-five hundred acres," was the reply.

"That big, huh?" Denny said, obviously impressed.

"Biggest around," Pat added.

"And how many head d'you run?"

"Normally around two thousand head," Pat answered. "Y'see, Pop's in the business of buyin' and' sellin' cattle. That's how he makes his dough. Right now we're way overstocked. Probably got us a good four thousand head on hand. And Pop's got orders for just about every last steer we've got. Only we couldn't ship th'm out. That fool range war came up and hog-tied us. Just to see what would happen, we tried runnin' out a small herd of about a hun-

31

dred head. We were jumped twice inside o' five miles from home. We lost fifteen head, all o' th'm shot dead, and a couple o' our hands got pretty well shot up too. We hotfooted it back. We tried the same thing twice again after that but we ran into trouble each time. So we quit. Now all we c'n do is stay put and hope this feuding stops so's we c'n get back into business again."

"How many times y'been raided?"

"Ohhh, five, six, maybe seven times all told."

"You an' Matt get mixed up in it when they hit you?"

" 'Course. Right now we're even. Each of us has four kills. Think I oughta get credit for five though. I hit one feller three times, but the others with him got him up on his horse. Even though he looked like he was about done for, I don't have 'ny way o' knowin' for sure if those three slugs I put in him killed him or if he's still alive."

"Think they'll try hittin' you again?" Denny asked.

"Yeah, sure. Pop says they must figger that if they keep carryin' the war to us that won't leave us free to go after them. So they figger it's safer an' smarter to raid us an' keep us on edge. F'r instance, last week they raided us three times. Fact that we keep killin' off one or two o' th'm each time and whittlin' them down doesn't seem to discourage th'm and stop th'm from takin' another whack at us an' still another."

"How come your Pa doesn't get sore and take a whack at them?" Denny wanted to know.

"Because he doesn't go for burning an' killing. Besides, he doesn't want to risk the lives of our hands. When we're hit, we're fighting back from behind cover, so the chances of any of us getting killed are pretty slim. And that's the way Pop wants it."

Suddenly, about half a mile away, was the most amazing sight that Denny's eyes had ever seen—a huge, compact mass of grazing cattle, and he stared wide-eyed and a little open-mouthed too. As his companions and he continued to lessen the distance between the herd and themselves, he became aware of rifle-armed horsemen walking their horses about as they scanned the open fields that spread away on every side of the grazing area. A mounted man, Big Matt McEntee, came loping toward them, and came together with them shortly, slacked a little in the saddle and thumbed his hat up from his forehead.

"What took you so long?" he asked, more patient than Denny had expected him to be. "Couldn't you tear yourselves away from the table?"

"It was my fault," Denny said. "I kept th'm back. Got talkin' to Kate and . . . "

McEntee did not give him a chance to finish. He wheeled his horse around, drummed back toward the herd, and cupping his hands around his mouth, yelled:

"All right, boys! They're here. So you c'n get going!"

There was instant response to his cry. Mounted men, sheathing their rifles, came swinging around the herd, drummed past the three youthful riders and headed for the house at a swift pace, an indication of their hunger and their eagerness to put something solid under their belts. After they had gone, Big Matt returned to the waiting trio.

"I appreciate what you boys are doing, spelling the crew so's they c'n get their grub," he began. "But it doesn't make sense, and I shoulda been the first one to realize it. So starting tomorrow morning we're gonna use the big wagon for a chuck wagon to lug the grub out here. That way the crew c'n eat on the job, half o' th'm eating while the other half stands guard. That's the way it used to be and the way it's gonna be all over again. Then there's another reason why we'll go back to a chuck wagon. I don't want you boys gettin' yourselves mixed up in any trouble that might pop up out here. So this is the last time for you boys. Now if you wanna space yourselves out and . . . "

"I'm old enough to be doing something worthwhile, Pop," young Matt said, interrupting his father. "It's something else again for Pat."

"The heck it is," the latter protested. "I'm only a mite younger'n you. But I'm just as big as you are and I c'n handle a gun just as good as you can and maybe even better."

"Whoa, you two," McEntee said, holding up his two big hands. "You wanna do something worthwhile? All right. You two take over for Lee Dibbs an' Eddie Ames in the barn. That'll give me two more experienced hands for guardin' our stock. All right?"

"S'matter with leavin' Dibbs and Ames where they are and lettin' us ride herd with . . . ?" young Matt began.

McEntee shook his head.

33

"Nope, no deal," he answered firmly. "Take what I offered you or turn it down. Now which'll it be?"

"You don't leave us much choice," Matt answered wryly.

His father grinned at him.

"That's right," he said. "That's the kind o' deals I like to make. The take it or leave it kind. Now if you an' Pat don't think much of the job I'm offering you, think this over. Your sister Kate's alone in the house and . . . "

"What about Ming?" Pat asked. "He counts too, doesn't he?"

"He sure does," McEntee replied quickly. "He's part o' the family. Same's Denny is."

The latter grinned a little.

"I was beginning to feel kind left out," he said. "I'm sure glad you feel I belong."

"You do, boy," Big Matt told him. "But lemme finish with Matt and Pat, then I'll get back to what I'm gonna expect of you. I'm looking to you two," and he looked squarely at his sons, "to see to it that Kate and Ming are protected. And if you don't think that's an important and worthwhile job, you've got another think coming. Now, you Denny. While Matt and Pat stand guard in the barn, you'll be in the houe or close to it, closer to Kate an' Ming than anybody else. So I'll be depending on you first off to see that nothing happens to either one o' th'm. All right?"

"Yeah, sure."

McEntee, obviously satisfied, sat back in the saddle. He settled his hat more firmly on his head.

"Now if you three wanna get moving and space yourselves out around the herd . . . "

The McEntee boys swung away and rode off in different directions. Denny loped away after Pat. When he saw the dark-haired youth pull up, he rode past him to a point about a hundred yards beyond him, reined in, and backing his horse off from the herd some twenty or thirty feet, wheeled him around and sat backturned to the grazing animals while he probed the flanking fields with his keen eyes. A horseman came toward him shortly. Denny shot a quick look at him. When he saw that it was McEntee, he relaxed. The big cattleman pulled up alongside of him.

"Wanted to tell you that you look fine," he began. "Even got your hair cut, huh?"

"Kate," Denny answered simply. Then he added: "The shirt, britches an' hat used to be Pat's. He outgrew th'm. The boots were Matt's."

"You care that they're hand-me-downs?"

"Nope," Denny replied without hesitation. "They're a heap better'n what I had. So I'm satisfied."

"When things settle down around these parts and get back to where they used to be, we'll ride into town, you, me and the boys, and we'll get us some new duds."

"Nope," Denny said quietly. "I gotta earn th'm or I don't want th'm." Then as an afterthought, he said: "Shoulda told you this before, only I didn't get the chance. So I'm sayin' it now. I'm sure obliged to you for takin' me in. But I don't like livin' offa you for free when I've got the money to pay part o' my way."

"Mean Jerry left you well fixed?"

"Dunno that I'd go that far."

"How far would you go?"

"How far will twenty-seven bucks take me?" Denny asked gravely.

"That's a lot o' money. When I was your age, fact is, a lot older'n sixteen, I didn't know what it was to have a whole buck that I could call my own. Yeah, twenty-seven bucks oughta take you quite a ways."

"Got it on me. Want me to give it to you now or wait'll we get back to the house?"

"I've got a better idea, boy. Why don't you give it to Kate to hold for you?"

"Y'mean you don't want it?"

Big Matt's blue eyes twinkled as he answered:

"I'm not runnin' a boarding house, and I don't take in anybody just like that. When I do, it's because that somebody happens to be somebody special, like Jerry McCune's boy who happens to be kin, a cousin. Your pa ever tell you about us before we came here, to this country?"

"Not too much. Why?"

"When Jerry an' me were kids, he was bigger'n me and anybody who picked on me had Jerry McCune to deal with. 'Course there were those who learned the hard way, and Jerry was always willing to teach th'm. We didn't have much. But what we had, we shared and shared alike. When we came here, we were still kids, and when our folks took off in different directions, there wasn't anything we could do about it. But Jerry an' me managed to keep track of each other over the years. I was always meaning to go look him up and see how he was doing, and if there was anything he needed. Guess I waited too long. I hit it right and if he didn't, if I'da known about it, he coulda had anything I had. Now let's get this understood between us, boy. You're part o' my family now, and my family doesn't owe me a thing for what I do for th'm. Aside from the fact that it's my job to do everything I can for th'm, I get a heckuva lot o' pleasure outta doing it. We get along right well, and I expect you to do what you have to to fit in with us. I don't think that's asking too much of you, d'you? You follow their lead, and when there's something I'd like you to do, and you do it because you want to do it and not because you feel it's, we-ll, your duty to do it, I'll never have 'ny complaints. That clear?"

"Yes, sir," Denny replied. "You mind tellin' me what I'm supposed to call you?"

"Matt," was the prompt answer. "That's what everybody else calls me. So you can too."

Denny nodded.

"All right for me to tell you just this once more, and I promise not to do it again being that you don't want me to, that I'm obliged to you and that I c'n tell you right here an' now that I'm gonna like living here?"

McEntee grinned at him, leaned over and patted him on the back, and straightening up, wheeled away only to swing around again to Denny's side.

"I owe you something like that I don't owe anybody else for," he said. "My life. Don't think I've forgotten that or that I ever will forget it."

"Heck," Denny said. "I think you're makin' more of a to-do about it than you oughta. Just happens that I was right there so I couldn't help but see that feller, that Marv Horton, fixin' to potshot you. Supposin' I hadn'ta got him first and that he'da got off a shot at you and missed?"

Big Matt shook his head.

"From that close up even Ming, who doesn't know
36

which end of a gun to hold, wouldn't've missed. So I know doggoned well that Marv wouldn't've missed either," he insisted. "Only reason I brought it up again was because I don't want you to think I'd forgotten what you did for me. That's all. See you later, boy. Half the crew will be back after supper to take over for us, and the other half takes over for them at midnight and gets spelled again at six in the morning."

With that McEntee rode off. The time passed slowly, so slowly in fact that around four o'clock or so Denny began to wonder if sundown would ever come. But it did eventually, after the longest unbroken afternoon of quiet that Denny had ever known. He found it to be more tiring than if he had been doing something that required physical effort. He assumed it was somewhere around six-thirty when four of the McE crew returned to relieve them. With Big Matt and Pat riding together and young Matt and Denny following them, they headed for home. Dibbs and Ames, with their rifles slung over their shoulders, were just coming down from the house when the four pulled up in front of the barn, dismounted stiffly and led their horses up the ramp and into the barn. Denny struggled to remove the heavy saddle from his horse.

He found a clean and freshly ironed shirt straddling the backrest of the chair when he entered his room. The water pitcher that stood in the middle of the matching bowl atop the washstand near the bureau was about three-quarters filled, while a clean towel and a fresh bar of yellow soap lay next to the bowl. Stripped to the waist, he had washed himself and was plying the towel vigorously over his body when he happened to glance at the door and noticed that he had left it ajar. Just as he was about to cross the room to close the door, he heard someone come up to it and he hastily retreated, whipping the towel around him and holding it close.

"You decent, Denny?" Kate asked.

"Got my pants on, if that's what you mean," he replied.

The door was pushed open a little wider, and Kate poked her head in at him.

"You ready for supper?"

"Just about."

She came inside, holding the door and looked at him.

37

"How'd things go? Anything happen?"

He shook his head.

"Nothing happened. Didn't have anything to do 'cept watch the cattle watchin' me, and wait for sundown. Oh, thanks for the shirt."

"Put it on," she instructed him, "so I can see how it fits. I found three more that look to be about the same size. If you can wear them, you'll have enough to get by with till you can get some new ones from town." When he made no attempt to come forward to get the shirt, she let go of the door, lifted the shirt off the chair and brought it over to him, held it out to him and said: "Take it and give me the towel."

"Haven't got my undershirt on yet," he said, a little lamely.

She drew back the shirt and said: "Well, put it on. You don't want to put it on over the towel, do you?"

"No," he said, and flushing a little, blurted out: "I don't think you oughta come in here when I'm gettin' dressed."

"Oh, fiddlesticks!" she retorted. "You've got your pants on, haven't you?" She snatched the towel away from him, ranged her eyes over him, and commented: "You aren't as skinny as I thought. Fact is, you aren't skinny at all."

"Get done," she commanded. "Don't want to keep the others waiting."

He turned to the bureau and took out a clean undershirt and pulled it over his head, pushed his arms through the sleeves and buttoned it up under her critical eyes.

Suddenly, Kate turned to him and asked: "You intend to get married some day?"

Denny looked at her. "I guess so. Bet you'll want to pick a wife for me. Be funny, wouldn't it, if you didn't like any o' the girls I take a shine to, and you're the only one left?"

"Get done," she repeated.

"I'd wind up having to marry you."

"I'm not so sure I'd want you," she retorted.

Taking the shirt from her, he put it on, and as he buttoned it up, he said:

"Y'mean that after all the trouble you'll have gone to makin' me over the way you want me to be, you're gonna let some other girl get me, some other girl who won't have done anything to . . . to deserve me?"

38

She didn't answer. He looked hard at her. There were tears in her eyes. Suddenly she turned her back on him and sniffled once or twice.

"Aw, c'mon now, Kate. Don't do that. Don't cry," he pleaded with her. "I was only teasin'. You oughta know I wouldn't say anything to hurt you." When there was no response from her, he went on with: "I owe you so much already, imagine how much I'm gonna owe you by the time I'm, say, eighteen or twenty?"

Her shoulders heaved a bit, a sign that she was still crying. He took advantage of her turned back to open his belt and hastily tuck in his shirttail and buckle his belt again. Then he moved up behind her, put his hands on her shoulders and gently turned her around. She averted her eyes.

"I wish I was older'n you instead o' you being older'n me," he told her in a low voice.

"What . . . what difference would that make?"

"Ohhh, it'd make a heckuva difference. Long's the boy . . . the man . . . is old enough, doesn't matter none how young the girl is." Then putting his lips against her ear, he asked in a whisper: "If I tell you how much I like you, will you get sore?"

"No," she whispered back, bowing her head against his shoulder.

"I like you a lot. Fact is, better'n anybody in the whole world. And when I'm old enough . . . "

"Go on," she urged him. "Tell me."

"Better if you just wait an' see. All I c'n tell you now is that you won't be disappointed. Till then you wanna be my girl?"

"If you want me to."

" 'Course I do."

"All right. I'll be your girl," she whispered, and this time she raised her head.

Now there was no sign of tears. Instead her eyes were bright and shiny.

"I've never kissed a girl before," he confided. He kissed her lightly on the lips, released her and stepped back from her. "Doesn't seem like I've only knowed . . . known you . . . for just one day. More like I've always known you. Seem that way to you too?"

39

"Yes."

He pecked at her lips a second time.

"I like kissin' you," he told her, and she smiled at him. "Look, you wanna go on downstairs while I get finished up?"

She nodded and turned to go.

"You won't be long, will you?" she asked over her shoulder as she headed for the door.

"No. No more'n a minute or so."

She went quickly out of the room. There was a small, square, wooden-framed looking glass on top of the bureau, and next to it lay a comb that he knew had to be one of Kate's. He dipped the comb in the water pitcher and tried to comb his cropped hair. But Kate had cut it so short, combing it proved futile, and he abandoned his efforts. A minute later he was on his way downstairs to the kitchen.

FIVE

Kate McEntee was the first to get up from the supper table. When she began to clear it, Ming, who was standing at the iron sink, made a half-turn, an indication that he was ready to receive and wash the dishes. Big Matt arose, and as all eyes followed him, sauntered across the kitchen to the back door, opened it and stood a little spread-legged in the doorway, staring out at the deepening darkness. He turned shortly and said:

"Think I'll ride out and see how the men are doing. Want you boys to keep your eyes open while I'm gone. When I get back, I'll spell you and you c'n turn in."

He didn't wait for anyone to say anything. He went out, yanking the door shut behind him. They heard his heavy, scuffing bootsteps briefly on the gravel path outside. Then they faded out. Young Matt got up, stifled a yawn with the back of his hand, and stretched mightily, rising up on his toes at the very top of his stretch.

Pat got up and followed his older brother out of the kitchen. When Denny heard them go upstairs, he lifted questioning eyes to Kate.

"They aren't turning in yet," she told him. "They post themselves with their rifles at the open windows in their rooms, ready to take a hand in the event of an attack."

"Oh!" Denny said, pushed back from the table and stood up. "What d'you think I oughta do?"

"Don't think there's anything in particular for you to do," Kate replied.

"Then I think I'll go outside and get some fresh air," he said, hitching up his pants. "How about you when you get done in here?"

"I've some sewing and darning to do."

"Have t'do it tonight? Can't it wait?"

" 'Fraid not."

He pushed back from the table and climbed to his feet. He was motionless for a moment, then he strode out of the room, went out of the house through the front door and stood in the deep shadows of the veranda. The night air was clean and crisp and he inhaled it deeply. Night light glinted briefly on the worn bars of the corral. Beyond it was the bunkhouse. He stood for a while, just looking around. A shadowy figure that he recognized at once as Kate emerged from the house and stood for a moment on the veranda, seeking him, he told himself. She finally spied him and came across it to his side.

"Changed your mind, huh?"

"Just felt the need for a breather."

When he curled his arm around her waist she did not protest. When he tightened his arm and sought to bring her closer so that he could kiss her, she stopped him with:

"Don't, Denny."

"Why? You're my girl, aren't you?"

"Yes. But that doesn't mean you have to kiss me every time I come near you."

"But I like to kiss you."

"Denny, there's a time and place for everything and . . ."

"And this isn't it, huh?"

"No, it isn't."

"Mean it's all right only when we're alone up in my room?"

She made no attempt to answer. Instead she said:

"This is the kind of night that the raiders wait for to come swooping down on us. So I suppose I'm a little edgy and nervous."

41

"Oh," he said, as though he understood, even though he didn't and was tempted to ask her what one thing had to do with the other. But he withstood the urge and said instead: "I see."

"Think I'll go back inside now."

"Yeah, maybe you oughta," he answered.

The darkness and the shadows in which they were standing made it difficult for him to tell for certain, but he thought she gave him an odd look as she turned and left him and went back into the house.

He crossed the veranda to the steps that led downward from it to the short path and perched himself on the next to the top step and sat hunched over with his chin cupped in his hands and his elbows resting on his knees and stared moodily into the darkness. He began to wonder if he had done the right thing in coming to Ludlow to live with the McEntees. Quite readily, though, he admitted that he had been warmly received and accepted by everyone; yet now, suddenly, he wasn't as happy about it as he had been earlier. He wondered if he wouldn't have been better off if there had been no Kate to take him under her wing, and if there had been only the male McEntees in the household. He was equally quick to acknowledge that Kate had already done a great deal for him. In spite of it, he was put out with her, and all because she hadn't let him kiss her. She was the one who had started the kissing business; if she hadn't, he knew he wouldn't have thought of it. He shook his head a little unhappily. He didn't understand it. Why had Kate let him kiss her one minute and reject his kiss the next minute?

He would make no further advances to her, he promised himself, and he would let her wonder about the change in his attitude. Maybe a display of indifference toward her would teach her something that she needed to be taught. While her mother had devoted so much of her time and herself to teaching her grammar and arithmetic and so on, she had neglected what to him was even more important. Kate would have to learn that by herself, and if she didn't, that would be her misfortune. She wasn't the only girl in the world. There were others, a lot of them too. And when he wanted one, he was sure he wouldn't have to look very far. He made another decision then too. He would stay on with the McEntees because there was no one else for him to turn to. But when he was older and able to shift for himself, he would go off on his own. There wouldn't be any ties to break, so there wouldn't have to be any tearful farewells. Just a simple statement of fact would do it.

He got up on his feet, stepped up on the veranda, retraced his steps across it to the front door and went inside. Through the portieres he glimpsed lamp light burning in the kitchen. However, the rest of the house appeared to be darkened. He mounted the stairs and trudged up. As he topped them he noticed that of the two wall bracket lamps on opposite sides of the landing, only one was lit. The wick in it had been turned down so low that only the barest bit of light showed in it, just enough to guide him down the landing. When he reached his room, he closed the door after him, groped for and located the bed, turned and seated hmself on the edge of it, took off his boots, and lay back across it with his legs and his stockinged feet dangling over the side. Clasping his hands behind his head, he lay staring up at the ceiling that he couldn't see because of the gloomy darkness. Despite his resolve to stay awake, even though he had already admitted to himself that he felt 'beat,' his tiredness and the sleep-inducing dark combined to overpower him. He struggled to keep his eyes open. But his struggles proved futile, and after a bit, he surrendered, his eyes closed and he dozed off. A sudden burst of gunfire from somewhere outside the house put an abrupt end to his short-lived sleep, and he awoke with a start and forced himself up into a sitting position, blinking and rubbing his heavy-lidded eyes with the backs of his hands. It took him a moment or two to know where he was. Riflefire boomed again and beat against the night. The raiders had struck again, he told himself, and the shooting meant that Dibbs and Ames had engaged them. He wondered if the four relief men in the bunkhouse were involved in the shooting.

He pulled on his boots, fumbled around till he found the buffalo gun, stood up, flung open the door and dashed out. Halfway along the length of the landing he heard more riflefire, only this time it came from somewhere closer at hand. Young Matt and Pat were shooting from the run-up windows of their darkened rooms, he decided. As he neared the stairs he heard a muffled, choked-off scream

43

from the direction of the kitchen.

He was about to start down when his keen ears caught the warning sound of faintly creaking bootsteps on the lower floor. Retreating, he bumped into the far side wall of the landing, suddenly whirled around and reached up and put out the wall light. He crept forward again to the head of the stairs and crouched down there with the buffalo gun leveled and holding on the stairs. A shadowy tip-toeing figure appeared at the foot of the stairs, paused there briefly, apparently listening for sounds of movement and activity on the upper floor, finally mounted the stairs and started up. Deliberately Denny held his fire, and held his breath too for fear of betraying himself to the intruder. When the latter was about halfway up and at such close range that it would have been impossible for Denny to have missed his target even with his eyes closed, he pulled the trigger. The buffalo gun exploded with such a deafening roar that it made him wince, and made his ears ring too. The shadowy figure was blown over backwards. Toppling out from the stairs, his body arched over and completed a perfect somersault. He struck the lowest step with a bone-breaking crash, caromed off and landed on the floor with a dull thud, and lay still.

Hastily reloading, Denny again started down the stairs, stepped on something that was hard and unyielding that he decided was the man's dropped gun, slowed himself when he neared the last step and barely managed to avoid trampling the sprawled-out body that lay just beyond the foot of the stairs. Wheeling around, he headed for the kitchen, halting just long enough to steal a quick look through the portieres. The lamp was still burning in there, but the room itself was deserted. Kate's sewing basket and a pile of clothing were on the table. One of the chairs lay on its side. Swinging around the table on the far side, Denny raced through the kitchen to the wide-open back door, noticing mechanically that thinned-out lamplight streamed out over the threshhold to a point a couple of feet beyond it. Denny peered out cautiously. Aside from two saddled horses that were idling together near one of the washline poles, there was no sign of anyone. Suddenly the sounds of scuffling reached him, and he quickly poked his head out for a look. Off to a side, almost against the back of the house

44

and about a stride or two from the end of the rear wall, were two struggling figures. One of them, Denny saw at once, was Kate, the other one, a man. Kate was sobbing hysterically as she sought frantically to break away from her captor, who was trying to drag her over to the waiting horses, neither of which showed any interest in what was going on so close by them.

Apparently changing her tactics, Kate clawed the man's face, and Denny, watching grimly and looking for an opportunity to get in a shot at him, heard him curse. When Kate suddenly lowered her head and butted him viciously, he let go of her for an instant. Quick to take advantage of the opportunity given her, Kate whirled around and fled houseward. Her captor ran after her. He was within lunging distance of her when Denny, with the buffalo gun raised and leveled, stepped out of the doorway. The roar that followed when he pulled the trigger drowned out an outcry from the man. Hit squarely, he stumbled to an awkward stop, turned and sagged against the pole nearest him, caromed off it and crumpled up on the ground.

Hastily shifting his gun to his left hand, Denny caught the sobbing Kate in the hollow of his right arm, and she clung to him and cried brokenly on his shoulder. A horseman came pounding up the gravel path, rounded the house in full flight and pulled his panting horse to a stiff-legged, sliding stop near the back door, and flung himself off the side-heaving animal. It was Big Matt McEntee.

"She hurt?" he wheezed at Denny.

"Nope. Scared out've her wits and a mite manhandled," was the boy's reply. "Aside from that, I think she's all right. You wanna take 'er?"

"Yeah, sure," the big cattleman answered quickly. He reached for his daughter, turned her around and took her in his arms and held her tight against him. "All right now, honey?"

"Yes," Kate said.

Suddenly bending and lifting her in his brawny arms while Kate curled her arms around his neck and pillowed her head on his shoulder, McEntee carried her into the house. Turning after them, Denny saw Big Matt pull a chair out from the table and ease himself down in it with Kate in his lap. There were running bootsteps overhead, then Denny heard them on the stairs. Suddenly there was a cry from the area of the stairway and the sound of someone falling.

"Denny," McEntee said without looking around at him. "You wanna go see what happened out there?"

Denny started around the table. He stopped in his tracks when young Matt, limping and favoring his left knee, and Pat, both of them rifle-armed, came into the kitchen.

"S'matter with her?" Pat asked.

"She's all right now," his father replied, looked up and asked: "One o' you take a header coming down the stairs?"

"Yeah, me," Matt said grumpily. "For a minute there, I thought I'd busted my leg."

Big Matt eyed him with concern.

"How's it feel now?"

"A little better. Musta given it something of a twist. But like I just said, it feels better. So I guess I'll live. Now would somebody mind telling me who doused the light on the landing and who that is layin' out there at the bottom o' the stairs? It was on account o' him and me not knowing he was layin' there that I took that spill."

"I put out the light," Denny said, and all eyes, even Kate's, focused on him. "When I heard somebody creakin' around down here near the stairs, I figgered I'd better get rid o' the light. When he came tip-toein' up the stairs, I cut down on him and blasted him off."

"Oh!" Matt said.

"Heard that cannon o' yours go off twice," Pat said. "The first time musta been when you plugged that maverick that Matt tripped over. Right? The second shot sounded like it came from outside the house. You get somebody with that shot too?"

Denny nodded and answered simply:

"Some feller who was tryin' to make off with Kate. He's layin' outside up against one o' the washline poles."

Pat grinned a little and said:

"You don't believe in wasting bullets, do you? You got Marv Horton with one shot and now these two tonight with one shot apiece."

"You don't understand, Pat," Big Matt said. "So I'd better straighten you out. Denny isn't tryin' to be economical. Fact is, that hasn't anything to do with it. Even though he's

46

kinda young to be handling a buffalo gun, or any other kind o' gun for that matter, he knows that all he has to do is hit a man just about anywhere's in the body, and that that's it. The man's dead as he'll ever be. So y'see it only takes one shot to do the trick. 'Course not everybody knows what a buffalo gun c'n do, or how to handle one. Denny does. Jerry musta showed him. Point is there's a knack to it and if you haven't got it, there's such a kick to it when it goes off, you don't come anywhere's near hitting what you're aimin' at and you wind up goin' one way and the gun another way. I told you what it did to Marv Horton, didn't I? That it just about tore the guts out've him?"

"How awful," Kate said, shuddering. She got up on her feet. "I think I've had more than enough for one night. So I'm going up to bed. Will one of you please put those things," and she pointed to the pile of clothes and the sewing basket, "on a chair for me?"

She started to round the table only to stop when Pat said:

"Hold it a minute, Sis. Better let me go make a light upstairs for you."

"And you'd better haul that . . . that character away from the stairs," Matt said.

Pat frowned and retorted:

"Thanks for telling me. I wouldn'ta thought o' that myself. I'da left him layin' there so's Kate could take a header over him like you did."

"How about me givin' you a hand?" Denny asked.

"Sure."

Denny propped up his gun against the wall and trudged out after Pat. Minutes later the two returned to the kitchen.

"All right, Kate," Pat announced.

"Good night," she said.

There was a chorused "G'night, Kate" in response. After she had gone, Pat turned to his father and asked:

"What d'you suppose they had in mind tryin' to grab off Kate?"

"Only one thing," Big Matt replied. "Green musta figgered that I'd come after her in one helluva sweat and that his gunnies would cut down on me and blast me good."

"What makes you think it was Green's outfit that hit us tonight?"

47

"Because it figgers it was. Now that Vic and Marv are dead, there aren't any more Hortons around to go on with this fool range war. Their crew didn't like either one o' th'm. So I don't think they felt that they owed Vic or Marv enough to try jumpin' us again on their own and risk gettin' themselves shot up. That's why I say it musta been Green's bunch."

"Denny!"

"Kate," Pat said, turning to Denny. "She wants you."

"Yeah," Matt said with a grin. "And you'd better hustle. She doesn't like to be kept waiting."

"Hope you didn't leave an o' your things layin' around," Pat added. "That's one thing she don't go for."

"Don't pay them any mind, boy," Big Matt said as Denny hurried out.

As he neared the stairs, Denny glanced at the dead man whom Pat and he had dragged over to the front door and whom they had left lying against it, backturned to the stairway. He raised his eyes as he started up the stairs. Kate was standing against the far wall. As he topped the stairs, he said:

"Yeah? You're all right, aren't you?"

"I'm still a little shaky. But I'm sure I'll sleep it off. I called you because I want to ask you something."

"Oh?"

"Denny, how many men have you killed?"

Her question surprised him. But he met her eyes and answered evenly:

"Six."

She stared at him through widened, horrified eyes, and a little open-mouthed too. She closed her mouth and gulped and swallowed hard.

"Doesn't it . . . doesn't it bother you?" she wanted to know in a shaken and faltering voice that was totally unlike her own. "You're only a boy. A sixteen-year-old boy, who's already killed six men. Doesn't the very thought of it horrify you?"

"No," he said as quietly as before. " 'Course I'm not proud of it so I don't go 'round braggin'. But same time I'm not ashamed of it either. Every last one o' those six got what was comin' to him. Way I see it, there wasn't any way outta any o' those killings for me. I didn't have 'ny . . . 'ny

48

choice. So I did what I had to."

"If I were the one who had killed those men, I don't think I could live with myself. Every waking minute and every sleeping minute too, I think I'd see their faces constantly before me, and I'd go out of my mind. But it doesn't bother you."

"Lemme ask you something, Kate. Would the fact that I've killed six men sound 'ny better to you if I was twenty-six or thirty-six, or even forty-six instead o' only sixteen?"

Ignoring his question, she said instead:

"What worries me is how many more will you have killed by the time you're a man?"

In turn he ignored her question, and said simply:

"The first three were the ones who murdered my Pa. The fourth one was that Marv Horton, and if I hadn'ta got him, your Pa wouldn't be sittin' downstairs talkin' to your brothers. He'd be in his grave, or bein' fixed up so's he could be buried. The fifth was that feller who's layin' downstairs near the door. If I hadn't' stopped him, d'you know what woulda happened? Sure as shootin', being that neither one o' your brothers heard him comin' up the stairs, he'da sneaked in on them one at a time and he'da killed both o' th'm. The last one was that feller you were wrestlin' around with outside and who was tryin' to make off with you. I don't suppose that any o' that means anything to you. All you c'n think of is that I'm a killer. What d'you want me to do, Kate? Want me to go get saddled up an' clear outta here? Y'know, a while ago I got to wondering if I hadn't made a mistake coming here, and if I shouldn'ta gone somewheres else. On my own of course. I'da made out somehow. If you want me to go, if you think it'll be easier on you not seein' me around, say so. What d'you say?"

She burst into tears.

"I don't know what I want you to do," she sobbed.

"Then I guess it's up to me to decide," he said quietly. " 'Bye, Kate. I'm sure obliged to you for everything you've done for me. I won't forget any of it. I'm sorry though that I turned out to be such a bust, such a disappointment to you. I didn't mean to. I want you to believe that. I hope you will. 'Bye."

He turned on his heel and went down the stairs.

Denny had just reached the lower floor when he heard a great sob burst from Kate. He turned and looked up in time to see her run toward her own room, and then he heard the door slam behind her. As he headed for the kitchen, the front door was shoved open; he stopped and looked back, saw the body that lay against it pushed back, enabling three men whom he recognized as members of the McE crew to enter. He watched them lift the dead man and carry him out, leaving the door ajar. Denny closed it and again headed for the kitchen. Pushing through the portieres, he was surprised to find it deserted. As he crossed the kitchen to the back door, he heard voices outside, and poked his head out. There were four figures standing around a horse across whose back a foot and hand-dangling body had already been lashed on. The second horse pawed the ground when one of the four, Pat McEntee, led the first one past Denny, rounded the house with him and led him away down the gravel path. Young Matt followed his brother with the second horse. The tallest of the two remaining figures, Big Matt, and a man whom Denny did not recognize but assumed was one of the McE crew, came toward the back door and stopped when McEntee saw Denny standing in the doorway.

"Somebody put my horse in the barn," McEntee said to the man with him. "Be a good feller, Jake, and saddle him up for me and leave him out front. I'll be along d'rectly."

"Right, Boss," Jake answered and trudged off.

"Thought you'd turned in, boy," Big Matt said to Denny. When there was no response, McEntee added: "We got three o' Green's outfit tonight, not just two. Third one was Nick Peters, Green's foreman. Jake Long, the man who was just here with me, was the one who got Nick."

"Uh-huh. What d'you do with th'm? I mean the dead ones?"

"Get rid o' th'm and pronto," was the prompt reply. "Don't want them layin' around and stinkin' up the place. Soon's I figger Jake's saddled up for me, I'll take them into town and leave th'm for Phil Gort, the butcher who does

50

our undertakin' too. He'll take care o' th'm."

"How about me doin' that for you? Nobody in town 'cept the sheriff knows me. So it'd be a heap safer for me to do it than for you, wouldn't it?"

"We-ll, now . . . "

"Besides," Denny continued, "I'll be heading that way, so it won't be putting me out any."

Big Matt looked hard at him.

"What d'you mean, you'll be heading that way?" he asked.

"I'm pullin' out," Denny replied.

"Oh, you are, huh? You've been here just one day. Fact is, it won't be a whole day till some time tomorrow morning, and just like that you suddenly decide you don't like it here and that you're leaving. Yet this afternoon when we were talkin', you told me you knew right then an' there that you were gonna like livin' here."

"That's what I thought then."

"But now you don't."

Denny didn't answer.

"What made you change your mind so all uva sudden? I don't like people, and that goes for sprouts too, who blow hot one minute and cold the next 'less they've got some pretty good reasons for it."

"Like I told you before, Matt, I'm obliged to you for takin' me in and tryin' to make me feel like I belong. Only it's come to me that I don't belong. I shoulda tried makin' a go of it on my own instead o' takin' the easy way and coming here right off."

McEntee shook his head and said:

"No good, Denny. You'll have to come up with something better'n that. You'd better come clean with me and tell me what's soured you on us. So start talkin' and you'd better say a whole lot if you expect to satisfy me."

"Aw, c'mon, Matt. Why can't you be satisfied with what I've told you instead o' making a big to-do about it?"

"I'm waitin' for you to start talkin', Denny," McEntee said firmly. "Kate have anything to do with this?"

"No," Denny lied. "Nobody had 'nything to do with this. Only me."

He flushed and hastily averted his eyes. But the towering

cattleman noticed it and deliberately proceeded to lead Denny into a betraying trap.

"I'm glad Kate didn't have 'nything to do with this," he said. "Oh, when she called you before, wasn't anything important she wanted, I don't suppose, huh?"

"No," Denny said, his face muscles tightening.

Big Matt promptly proceeded to close the trap.

"I know the boys like you and I think you like them," he said evenly. "And from what Kate told me, I took it that you an' she were hittin' it off. I don't think it coulda been the boys who got you to change your mind about stayin' on here. So it figgers it musta been Kate. You wanna tell me all about it, Denny, or d'you want me to call Kate down here?"

Too late Denny realized what had happened.

Unhappily he said: "Don't call her. I'll tell you."

Without any embellishment because he had yet to learn about guile, he related his conversation with Kate. McEntee held his steady gaze on him throughout. Not once did he interrupt him.

"She took on so," Denny said, "she made me feel like I was a reg'lar killer, like I enjoyed killing. I tried explaining to her, tried to show her that in every one o' those six killings, I didn't have 'ny . . . 'ny choice. But all she did was cry, and the more she cried, the worse I felt. So I decided there wasn't anything else for me to do 'cept cut out. I figgered that when she didn't see me around, she'd forget about me and she'd feel better."

"That's the whole story?"

"Uh-huh," Denny said, nodding. "Now there's only one thing that bothers me."

"What's that?"

"You'll say something to Kate and it'll make her feel even worse'n she does now, and I wouldn't want that to happen. I owe her a lot, and I like her a lot too. Now I'm wondering if it wouldn'ta been better all around, specially for Kate, if I hadn'ta waited to say goodbye to you, and if I hadda gone straight down to the barn, mounted up and headed out."

"I'm glad you didn't, Denny. I wouldn't have liked that. Look, you wanna ride into town with me?"

"Yeah, sure."

"Then suppose you go on down to the barn and get saddled up," McEntee instructed him, "and wait there for me. I won't be long." He followed Denny inside. But when the boy reached for his gun, Big Matt stopped him and took it himself and said: "I know you won't go off without this thing. So just to make sure you won't, I'll hang on to it for now."

Denny did not protest. Instead he asked earnestly:

"When you talk to her, go easy with her, will yuh, Matt?"

McEntee smiled and answered:

"I owe her a lot too, Denny, for fillin' in for her Ma and for doing such a swell job of runnin' this house and us. And like you, I kinda like her too. So you oughta know I wouldn't even think of sayin' or doin' anything to hurt her."

"Thanks," Denny said simply.

With Denny marching ahead and Big Matt carrying the buffalo gun, they trooped out of the kitchen. When they came to the stairway, they parted wordlessly, McEntee turning and plodding a little wearily and heavy-legged up the stairs while Denny walked on, left the house through the front door and tramped down toward the barn. As he lifted his gaze to it, he could make out three shadowy figures idling in front of it, and close by them, a saddled horse that he assumed was McEntee's. A dozen feet away on the far side of the ramp were three horses. As he came closer, the three figures dissolved into Matt and Pat McEntee and Jake Long, while another look at the waiting horses revealed the bodies of the dead men draped over the animals' backs and lashed on. As Denny neared the barn, Pat turned and called to him.

"Goin' somewhere, Denny?"

"Uh-huh," Denny replied. "To town with your Pa. Takin' them in," and he pointed to the dead men.

"How about us trailin' along?" Matt asked.

"Your Pa'll be along d'rectly," Denny told him. "Supposin' you ask him?"

As Denny stepped up on the ramp, Jake Long said:

"You wanna watch it, young feller. Liable to be some o' Green's gunnies in town and when they see them," and he

53

jerked his head in the direction of the dead men, "there'll
be hell to pay."

Denny didn't answer. He trudged up the ramp and went
into the barn. A rifle-armed man, Lee Dibbs, emerged from
the shadows at the rear. When he saw Denny, he said:

"Put your saddle up in the hay loft and dug up a real
light one for you to use. You'll find it ridin' that wooden
horse."

Denny nodded and acknowledged with a simple:
"Thanks."

Dibbs grinned and said: "Just a part o' the service."

Denny was saddling up when he heard louder voices outside. As he was tightening the belly cinches, Jake Long
came into the barn and said to him:

"Boss wants me to go along too."

"What about the boys?"

"Told them to stay put in the house and keep an eye out
till we get back."

"Oh!"

"Hear tell you're right handy with a gun. Didn't see one
on you when you came in here. Leave it up at the house?"

"Big Matt's got it."

"Oh!" Long said. As he turned away to get his horse, he
said over his shoulder: "I'll be along in a couple o'
minutes."

"I'll be outside."

When Denny emerged from the barn leading his horse,
he found Big Matt mounted and waiting. He shot a look in
the direction of the house and caught a glimpse of Matt and
Pat going up the veranda steps. As he hoisted himself up
into the saddle, McEntee handed him the buffalo gun, and
said:

"Got everything straightened out for you with Kate."

"Oh? She sore because I told you?"

"Nope. She figgered you would before you rode off. Feel
better now?"

"Yeah, sure," Denny answered, settling himself a little
more comfortably in the saddle and hand-holding his gun
across his knees with his right hand, took the reins in his
left. "Thanks for talkin' up for me, Matt."

"Any time, boy."

Hoofs thumped hollowly on the ramp just then and Jake

Long rode down its sloping length to join them. Denny had already noted that there was a riflebutt jutting out of McEntee's saddleboot; he spotted one in Long's boot too.

"Take the lead line, Jake," Big Matt instructed the lanky puncher, "and fall behind us."

"Right, Boss," Jake acknowledged and pulled away from them, walked his mount over to where the horses with the dead men were waiting, got down and bent over and came erect again almost at once with a length of rope in his hand, climbed up astride his own horse, looped the line around his pommel and said simply: "All set, Boss."

"Let's go," McEntee said and wheeled away from the barn. Denny wheeled after him and ranged up alongside of him as they headed for the archway and the open road beyond it. Turning to him, Big Matt said: "Be glad when this is done and we're back home again. I haven't been gettin' anywhere's near enough sleep lately and it's beginning to ketch up with me. I'm tuckered out. Feel like I could sleep for a week."

"Still don't see why I couldn'ta done this job for you," Denny answered. "You coulda stayed put and got yourself some rest instead o' having to make this long ride goin' and comin'. You've still got time to turn around an' go back to the house, y'know."

"No," the big cattleman said. "Better for me to be along with you an' Jake."

Denny did not pursue the matter. It was up to McEntee to decide for himself, and since he had, there was no point in arguing. They jogged through the archway. When they reached the road, they turned eastward. The road was oppressively, almost ominously silent, and so gloomily dark that Denny could not even see his own hand in front of his face. Suddenly he realized that the gloom was due to the thickly-branched trees that lined the roadside. Taking the lead from McEntee, the horses broke into a trot. Denny twisted around and looked back. Long and the three horses that he was leading were drumming along at a fairly even pace.

Turning to McEntee who was riding within touching distance of him, Denny said:

"Jake says there's a chance that some o' Green's gunnies might be in town, and that we're liable to have trouble with

55

th'm when they see what we're bringin' in with us."

"Too late for them to be there," Big Matt answered. "If it was earlier, they probably would be around. But not this time o' night because the saloon closes around ten, week nights."

"That's where you're wrong, Boss," Jake said from so close to them that both McEntee and Denny turned and looked back and were surprised to find the lanky puncher riding directly behind them. "If there's anybody around who wants to drink, Al Gerling'll stay open. He isn't one to let the hour stop him from takin' in an extra couple o' bucks."

There was no response, no comment, from McEntee and no further conversation most of the rest of the way to town. When they emerged from the trees, the deep gloom disappeared. But it was slow going due to the trotting pace that had to be imposed, lest the lashed on bodies be jolted, slip and topple off the horses that were carrying them. The miles dropped away slowly behind them, and the ride that should not have taken any more than twenty or possibly twenty-five minutes at the most took more than an hour. Suddenly McEntee looked up and announced:

"There she is, about a mile or so ahead of us."

"Yeah," Jake agreed, and added a bit wryly: "Only y'see some kind o' light above the town, Boss? You know what that means, don't you?"

" 'Course I do," Big Matt retorted in a sharper tone than he usually used. "That's the reflection of the lights from the saloon. Means it's still open."

"Right," Jake said.

"So instead o' ridin' straight in," McEntee said, "we'll go 'round the back way to Gort's place. And when we dump them off," obviously referring to the dead men even though he neither pointed to them nor indicated them in any way, "we'll head out the same way. Ord'narily I won't turn tail an' run from anybody. 'Specially from an outfit like Milt Green's. But with the odds against us, I'm not lookin' to take them on in a shoot-out."

There was no comment from either of his companions. When they came to within a hundred yards or so of Ludlow and had halted abreast of the entrance to the town, they noticed that the saloon was the only establishment that was

56

still open. It was ablaze with yellowish lamplight. Some of the light streamed out through the wide-open doors, spanned the narrow walk and reached beyond the low curb, and played over the legs of some six or eight horses that were tied to the hitchrail in front of the place.

"C'mon," McEntee said, and Denny and Jake Long followed him away. When they reached the open backyards of the buildings that fronted on the street, they wheeled and jogged past them till Big Matt said, low-voiced: "That's Gort's place. The one right ahead of us."

"He's still up," Denny said. "There's a light burnin' upstairs."

When they wheeled again and pulled up at Gort's back door, Long asked:

"D'we get down or stay put?"

"Stay put," he was told.

One of the horses snorted and tossed his head. A curtained window, the one through which light sifted out, was run up and a man poked his head out.

"Who's down there?" he asked.

"Sh-h. Keep your voice down, Gort," McEntee told him in a guarded tone.

"Who are you an' what d'you want here this time o' night?"

"Never mind for now who I am. Leavin' three customers for you to fix up. You don't hafta do it tonight. They c'n wait till tomorrow."

"They your men?"

"Nope. Milt Green's."

"Milt Green's, huh? Don't leave th'm. Take th'm somewhere's else. I don't want any part o' them or him. Last time somebody brought in one o' his hands and I fixed him up, laid him out nice an' proper, Green wouldn't pay me. Told me 'less he himself tells me to do a job for him, not to take anybody else's say-so and to turn it down. So that's what I'm doing. Take them away from here, mister."

"Told you to keep your voice down," McEntee said a second time. "Now what am I gonna do with three dead men?"

"Don't ask me," Gort answered. "I didn't kill th'm. You did. So you figger that one out for yourself."

"How much d'you want to do the job on th'm?"

"Twenty-five bucks and cash in advance."

"Twenty-five bucks?" Big Matt repeated. "You locoed or something? Give you ten bucks, and you c'n take it or leave it."

"I'm leavin' it!" the butcher yelled. "Keep your ten bucks and take those dead ones the hell away from here, or I'll go call the law!"

McEntee muttered something under his breath. But he did not answer Gort. Instead, half-turning his head, he said out of the side of his mouth:

"We're leavin' them here whether Gort likes it or not. Drop that lead line, Jake. Then you an' Denny back away from here and ride like hell for home. I'll be right behind you."

"Hey, you're McEntee, aren't you?" Gort yelled. "Kinda thought so before only I wasn't sure. But I am now. I dunno what you're fixin to do down there, but I'm warning you . . ."

"Go ahead, you two," Big Matt said quietly. "Get going."

Jake and Denny backed their horses, wheeled them, and lashing them with the loose ends of the reins, sent them pounding away. McEntee wheeled around too and dashed after them. Gort yelled a third time but the thumping hoof-beats drowned him out. Big Matt saw Denny and Jake cut past the corner and take the road that led to the McE. At the same time he saw a band of mounted men appear at the corner and swing northward, confirming his belief that the tied-up horses belong to Green's crew, because they were heading in the direction in which Green's spread was located. They pulled up abruptly and one of them yelled something that the two fleeing riders ignored. When the band swung around and set out after them, a couple of the men snapping shots at them, McEntee cursed and hauled out his rifle. Urging his horse on faster, he cut between the mounted men and their quarries, flung a couple of shots at Green's men, and flashed away. In a matter of minutes he overtook Denny and Long.

"Faster!" he yelled to them and twisted around with his rifle raised, ready for a quick shot. "I'll hold th'm off!" he shouted, as they went past him.

One of the pursuing horsemen, outdistancing his companion and ranging ahead, pegged a couple of shots at the fleeing trio. McEntee promptly fired back at him. There was another exchange of shots, and Big Matt, hit solidly, gasped and sagged brokenly in the saddle, dropped his rifle, and fell forward with his arms curled around his horse's neck. Somehow he managed to hang on and maintain his seat astride the swift-running horse. Jake Long looked back, and pulled up, and waited for McEntee's mount to come alongside of him. Moving in as close to his employer as he could, and leaning far out of the saddle, he reached out and got a grip on Big Matt's shirt and helped keep him on his horse's back.

"Denny!" he yelled. "Boss is hit! Y'better gimme a hand with him!"

Instantly Denny reined in. He permitted Jake and McEntee to pass him, then dashing after them, came up on Big Matt's left side and moving in close to the badly injured man, did what he could to help keep him in the saddle. The horseman who had bested McEntee in the exchange of gunfire came into view and fired twice at them. Denny dropped back and swung around with the buffalo gun half-raised. The man was coming on swiftly. He was about thirty feet away when Denny's curled finger pulled the trigger. The gun went off with a thunderous roar. Horse and rider plunged to the ground. Wheeling around again, Denny galloped after Long and McEntee. Several times he looked back. But there was neither sound nor sight of their pursuers.

Dibbs and Ames came hurrying out of the barn in response to Denny's cry to them. At his insistence, they dropped their rifles in the churned-up dirt at the foot of the ramp and ran along with him up to the house. In front of it they found Jake, who had already dismounted, actually struggling to stop the now unconscious and limp-bodied McEntee from toppling off his horse. The side-heaving animal looked around, apparently wondering what was going on. The three men eased Big Matt down and carried him up the path to the veranda steps, shifted their burden a bit, got him up to the veranda and across it and into the house. Denny who had scurried inside ahead of them to
59

summon the McEntee boys followed them when they came dashing down the stairs. Then with Denny looking on, the three men and the two youths carried Big Matt up to his room and laid him in his bed.

"There a doctor in town?" Denny asked Pat.

The dark-haired, grim-faced youth, shook his head.

"Used to be," he replied. "But he cleared out right after the trouble began."

Standing around the motionless figure in the bed, they watched silently as Jake Long, who gave evidence of having had experience with gunshot wounds, unbuttoned McEntee's bloodied outer shirt and then his equally blood-stained undershirt and bared his chest. Jake bent over him, took one look at the bullet hole in the unconscious cattle-man's chest, shook his head, and straightening up, pointed to it mutely. The others moved closer to the bed and peered hard at it too. Then they moved back a bit. Turning to young Matt, Jake said:

"Hit bad. No doctor could do anything for him. Just a matter o' time now. Minutes, maybe even an hour. But no more'n that."

"How . . . how did it happen?"

"Some o' Green's outfit were in town. They came after us when we were hightailin' it for home. Your Pa and one o' th'm swapped shots. That's how it happened. Denny," and he nodded at the boy who was standing on the opposite side of the bed, "got him, the feller who shot your Pa. Blasted him an' his horse right smack in the middle o' the road."

"Think I'll go wake Kate," Pat announced, and everyone looked at him. "She oughta be told."

No one said anything. Moving around the bed, Pat went out of the room. Again Long bent over Big Matt, and peered closely into his face. Suddenly a quiver ran through the big man's body and his left leg jerked convulsively. A sigh that must have come from deep down inside of him slipped through his slightly parted lips. It was a sign that his breath and his life were ebbing out of him. Then he lay still again. Still half-bent over him, Jake turned his head and looked at young Matt.

"That's it," he said and added simply: "He's dead."

He pulled the blanket out from under McEntee's body,

60

drew it all the way up, and covered the dead man's face and head. With Dibbs and Ames following him, he led the way out of the room. Deciding that he did not belong in there either, that the dead man should be left to his sons and daughter, Denny trudged out too. As he neared the stairs and turned to go down, the front door closed behind Long and the other two punchers. He made his way down and slowly entered the kitchen, pulled out a chair from the table and slumped down in it.

SEVEN

They sat around the big table in the kitchen, Denny on one side of it, the two McEntee youths on the other, all of them grim-looking and silent, each thinking his own unhappy thoughts. To Denny, Big Matt McEntee's untimely death meant the loss of a good and understanding friend who because of his link to the past, Jerry McCune, had become Denny's link to the McE. With Big Matt gone, he wondered if he should stay on. While he felt certain that the boys liked him, he was just as certain that they would not do what their father had done, undertake to smooth things out between Kate and him. We-ll, he told himself, he wouldn't make the break without first seeing what developed.

Finally Pat stirred himself and sat up, moved in closer to the table, folded his arms and leaning over them, asked:

"What are we gonna bury him in, Matt?"

"I've been wondering about that too," the latter replied, raising his eyes to meet his brother's. " 'Course we oughta have a coffin only I don't think it'd be safe for any of us to make the trip into town to get one."

"How 'bout me goin'?" Denny asked.

The two McEntees looked at him. It was Matt who answered with a shake of his head.

"No, Denny. It's swell of you to offer. But you aren't gonna take a chance o' gettin' yourself plugged any more'n any one of us is. For the time being we'll hafta roll Pop up in canvas and bury him in that. 'Course when things get back to . . . to normal . . ."

"If they ever do," Pat interrupted bitterly.

61

"You don't think there's any chance o' that now that your Pa's gone?" Denny asked.

Pat's shoulders lifted in a shrug.

"Who knows? Pop didn't start this fool range war. They did, Green, Horton and those other lousy two-bit outfits that didn't like it when we, Joe Lombard, Tom Hill and Steve Parker fenced in our properties so that the others couldn't drive their herds over our lands to the railroad or to water even though the water is well inside our spreads, actually between all four o' th'm. That's when it started, with them cutting our fences. When we drove them back and restrung the fences, the shooting started. Since Pop wasn't the leader among the bigger cattlemen, the fact that he's dead doesn't mean that the others will be willing to kow-tow to the small fry and let them ride roughshod over us. Hill and Lombard are tough fighters. For that matter, so's Parker. Lombard an his crew even carried the fighting to some of those two-bit characters who tried to break through the Box-L and burned out a couple of th'm."

"Because we didn't go after those small fry," Matt added, "they thought Pop was a-scared o' th'm. That's why they kept takin' whacks at us."

"Then you think it'd be all right to forget about the coffin for now and use canvas, huh, Matt?" Pat asked his older brother.

Matt nodded.

There were light approaching footsteps and presently Kate McEntee, holding a warm robe closely around her, her night dress showing below it and her feet slippered, came into the kitchen. Denny reached out, pulled out a chair for her and she sank down in it. Ignoring Denny, she looked across the table at her brothers.

"We've got to make plans," she announced evenly. "And the sooner the better."

"We'll go on same's Pop did," Matt told her. "So what plans do we need?"

"Might be a good idea to make Jake Long foreman," Pat suggested, "and let him run things. He's been so close to Pop and for so many years, he knows exactly what Pop did and why."

"Yeah," Matt conceded. "Might be a good idea for us to do that. Leastways, think about it."

"Of course we know where Pa should be buried," Kate said.

" 'Course," Matt said. "Next to Ma."

"What about a coffin?" Kate asked.

Matt told her what Pat and he had decided. Her expression reflected her disapproval.

"I'll go to town for the coffin," she announced. "When it gets light, one of you hitch up the wagon for me. When I get back, we'll attend to the burial."

"I don't like the idea of you goin' into town alone," Pat said.

"I don't either," Matt said.

"Denny offered to go into town for the coffin," Pat told his sister.

She bristled and retorted:

"And have him get into a fight with someone and add another killing to the list he's already built up?" She turned so suddenly upon Denny, taking him by surprise, that he felt his face crimson. "You've been here one day. But it's been an awf'lly busy one for you, hasn't it? You'd killed three men before you got here, then one this morning and two more tonight. That made it six. Did you add any to that number while you were in town with my father?"

"No," Denny replied. "But on the way back."

She stared at him with wide eyes.

"The one who shot your Pa," he told her quietly. "He kept comin' after us and kept shooting. Jake was busy holdin' up your Pa. So it was up to me to do something to stop him so's we both could keep him up on his horse and get him back here quick's we could and without lettin' anybody hold us back."

"So you killed him."

Denny did not answer her.

"He's only a boy, sixteen years old," she said, turning away from him and again addressing herself to her brothers, "and already he's killed seven men. How many d'you think he will have killed by the time he's twenty-one? Or even your age, Matt, or yours, Pat?"

"Aw, come on now, Kate," Matt protested, "You're lookin' at this all wrong."

"You make it sound like, we-ll, like he goes outta his way to kill people," Pat chimed in with, "and you know blamed well he doesn't do anything of the kind. Things happen and Denny finds himself caught in the middle o' th'm and he has to do something to . . . to protect himself or this morning it was Pop, then tonight it was Matt and me, and then it was you."

"I expected you two to defend him," Kat replied. "Pa did too. It happens though that I don't approve of young boys carrying or using guns, and the very thought of a boy of Denny's age killing anyone sickens me."

"You didn't make such a to-do about it," Matt pointed out, "When you heard that if it hadn'ta been for Denny Mary Horton woulda killed Pop."

"Yeah, then it didn't sicken you, did it?" Pat added. "If Pop was alive now, he'd tell you to leave Denny be. And I think you oughta."

"Pa did tell me that, and just this evening too," Kate acknowledged. "He also told me what he'd told us so many times before, that he owed Denny's father more than he could ever repay. Very well. For his sake, and because he insisted that this was now Denny's home in view of Pa's indebtedness to Jerry McCune and to Denny too, that's the last I'll ever say on the subject. Denny can go on killing as freely as before, and you two can defend and protect him. As for me, I'm washing my hands of him completely."

"Thanks for talkin' up for me," Denny said, looking across the table to Matt and Pat. "You won't have t'do it again though." The two opposite him lifted questioning eyes to him. "I'll stay around till after you bury your Pa. Then I'll saddle up and clear out."

"No call for you to do that," Matt said.

"That's right, Denny," Pat said. "Kate doesn't mean half o' what she says. So all you have t'do is give her a little time and she'll get over it."

Denny met Pat's eyes, and shook his head and said with finality:

"No. I don't belong here. While I'm obliged to all o' you for takin' me in and tryin' to make me believe I belong here, I don't. Told that to your Pa and to Kate too, same's I told th'm both that I shouldn'ta come here even though my Pa wanted me to. I shoulda gone off on my own."

There was no response, nothing at all from his listeners who continued to hold their gaze on him. Without a word he arose and marched out of the kitchen, tramped upstairs and went into his room. He groped his way to the bureau. There were some matches in the top drawer. He fumbled around in it till he found one, scratched it on his pants leg, and when it flamed, he made a light in the lamp, blew out the scorched matchstick and laid it on the washstand. He hauled his saddlebags out of the clothes closet, opened them and drew out a small sack of bullets for the buffalo gun and the holstered gun that he had taken from the shifty-eyed man whom he had encountered on the range, and tossed them on the bed. Afraid that the foodstuffs that remained uneaten in the bags had gone bad, he took them downstairs, ignoring the questioning eyes of the McEntees, and dumped the edibles in the swill barrel outside the back door, and again ignoring the McEntees, retraced his steps through the kitchen and up the stairs to his room. From the neat and orderly little piles of shirts and underwear in the second drawer of the bureau he took a couple of each, folded them and stowed them away in the saddlebags, tucked in the sack of bullets, took out a handful of them and stuffed them in his pants pocket, lifted his father's gun-belt off the bedpost and managed to squeeze it in too. He caught up the other holstered gun from the bed, wrapped the belt around the gun and laid it on the bureau. He had no need of it. One of the McEntees would find use for it, he told himself. He seated himself on the edge of the bed, lay back across it, squirmed a bit as he got himself into a comfortable position, and sighed. Then despite the rays of lamplight that shone on him, his eyes closed and he dozed off.

He had no idea how long he had been sleeping when a startling, window-rattling roar of gunfire woke him. His eyes opened, but he did not move. Instead he lay there listening to the shooting and thinking to himself:

"Second time tonight. Those blamed raiders don't know when to quit. 'Less it's another outfit and not the same bunch that hit us earlier tonight."

Reluctantly he forced himself up into a sitting position, rubbed his eyes, yawned and stretched, and sat hunched over on the bed.

"All I'd hafta do," he thought bitterly to himself, "would be to grab my gun 'n go hustlin' outta here and lend the

65

boys a hand fightin' off those pesky raiders. Kate'd have a fit." Now he heard riflefire from close by. It meant that the McEntee boys were bringing their rifles into play from the windows of their individual rooms. He sat upright when he heard a windowpane shatter and fall in with a crash.

The firing continued, swelled at times and fell off for a brief moment or two and suddenly broke out again and reached a thunderous pitch. Twice he was tempted to grab his gun and dash out regardless of Kate and of what she would have to say. He liked Matt and Pat and felt that they in turn liked him. Proof of it was the fact that they had gone back at Kate in their defense of him. He got up and walked to the door and stood listening in the open doorway.

"Kate!" he heard someone yell, and Denny recognized the voice. It was Matt's. "They're fixin' to rush the house! Get downstairs to the cellar and lock yourself in, y'hear? Hustle it now!"

"I hear!" Kate answered.

Whirling around he caught up his gun and bolted out. As he neared the stairway, a door was flung open, and Kate, fully dressed this time, came racing down the landing.

"They're going to rush the house!" she cried to him.

"I know. I heard Matt same's you did." When they came together at the stairway and she made no attempt to break past him and scamper down, he asked her: "Well? What are you waiting for? Why don't you get outta here like Matt told you?"

"Come with me!"

"No. I've got something to do here, and it doesn't matter how you feel about it. I'm still gonna do it."

"You hate me now, don't you?"

"I don't hate anybody. You or anybody else."

"You hate me! I can tell by the way you're looking at me."

He moved away from her and turned out the light, plunging the landing into gloomy darkness. He hurried down the stairs and bolted the front door, whirled around and ran through the kitchen to the back door, bolted that one too, and slung a couple of chairs against it. If the raiders succeeded in breaking in, they would fall over the chairs in the darkness. He jumped up on a chair and by stretching managed to reach the ceiling lamp and turned out the light. He dragged a couple of other chairs out with him, overturned them and scattered them about between the front door and the stairway. Then he ran back to the kitchen and brought back two more chairs, toppled them over on their sides and left them where they fell around the door. Then retreating, carefully, though, so as to avoid taking a spill for himself over the obstacles that he had provided for the raiders, he reached the stairway without mishap, backed up the steps to the landing, and turning, promptly collided with someone and trampled her.

"Don't stand around out here!" he told Kate a little crossly. "Go back to your room or to mine and douse the light and get down on the floor. But stay away from the window. If they start peggin' shots at it, flyin' glass c'n do you as much hurt as a bullet c'n, maybe even more. G'wan now!"

He pushed her off, turned and crouched down at the head of the stairs with his gun holding on the front door. The handful of bullets in his pants pocket made a hard, sizable lump. He stiffened a little when he heard booted footsteps on the veranda, raised his gun the barest bit higher and curled his finger around the trigger. Someone came up to the door, tried it, and finding it locked, put his shoulder to it and tried to force it. But the sturdy door refused to give way to him. There were more bootsteps on the veranda, and an indistinct murmur of voices, and Denny took that to mean that another man had joined the first one. Together they put their shoulders to the door. When they failed to budge it, they must have backed off from it and then hurled themselves at it. This time the door could not withstand them. The bolt fell on the floor and the forced door flew open. Denny heard a chair scrape on the floor as it was pushed back by the door. He glimpsed two tall shadowy figures a step or so inside the doorway. The buffalo gun exploded with a deafening roar that shook the house, and one man was actually blown out while his companion, obviously hit too but not as seriously, gasped aloud, stumbled forward and sprawled heavily over a chair. Denny heard him curse. As the intruder dragged himself, he flung a badly aimed shot in the direction of the stairway. Denny heard the bullet strike the banister rail somewhere below him. The buffalo gun thundered a more authoritative and a far more accurate answer. Apparently solidly hit this time, the hapless man's legs must have buckled under him as he went careening backward out of the house. Denny heard him fall on the veranda.

Rifle and pistol fire beat again against the night, and the sound of approaching horses' hoofs lifted and carried above the din. Hastily reloading, and a little uneasy now as he awaited a concerted rush upon the darkened house, his head jerked around when he heard another pane of glass shatter and crash under the piercing impetus of a bullet, and he looked in the direction of his room. Suddenly he leaped up and ran down the landing and stumbled to a stop outside the open doorway. Kate had obeyed him and had turned out the lamplight.

"Kate," he called. "You all right?"

"Yes," came her reply, and because her voice sounded somewhat muffled, he wondered about it. "I'm under the bed."

"Oh!" he said. "That's good. Heard another window fall in and I wondered if it was in here."

"It was. It was the most frightening thing I ever heard. Don't come in here, Denny. There must be broken glass all over the place."

"Uh-huh. Stay put where you are," he instructed her. "Leastways till this thing is over and we c'n make a light so's you c'n see what you're crawlin' around in. Gotta go, Kate."

"Denny," she called after him as he turned to hurry back to his post.

He stopped in his tracks and stood head-turned.

"Yeah?"

"Be careful, please."

"Oh, I'm careful, all right. Only I think you oughta know this now. Two men broke in the front door. I got both o' th'm. Dunno for sure if I killed both or only one. If you wanna make a to-do about it, go ahead. Won't matter much though. Like I told the boys a while ago, right after you bury your Pa, I'll be leavin' here."

He did not wait to hear her response. He scurried back to the head of the stairs and knelt down. Three men, as shadowy as the first two, appeared in the open doorway. At the same time he heard the back door burst open, heard a

68

couple of the chairs that he had slung against it scrape on the kitchen floor, and heard some of the incoming raiders fall over them. He raised his gun and fired at the shadowy figures in the doorway. The blast made him wince. The three men melted backward into the darkness. Then two of them came bounding in only to crash into the overturned chairs. But they were smarter than the two who had forced the door; they used the chairs they had fallen over as shields and opened fire on the stairway. Their bullets tore into the steps and splintered some and gouged out chunks of wood from others. Denny replied to their fire. One man got up on his feet and, turning himself, sagged against the door jamb, huddled there for a brief moment, then forcing himself up, lurched out and disappeared. Then there was a rush of booted feet from the direction of the kitchen. Guns that were poked through between the banister uprights belched fire at Denny, who hastily retreated from the stairway, flattening out on the landing floor on his belly. A bullet struck and smashed the wall lamp just beyond him, the broken bits of glass tinkling on the floor within touching distance of him. There was a concerted rush for the stairs. Just then, two figures, Matt and Pat McEntee, came dashing down the landing, and crouching down near Denny, fired into the huddled figures at the foot of the stairs. Driven back, one of the raiders flung a last shot upward as he backed off. Denny, half-raised up and with his gun ready for another shot, gasped when hot iron seared seared his head. He sagged face downward on the floor and lay still.

Bright, cheerful sunlight sifted into the bedroom through the curtain and the rather thin-worn window shade that someone had drawn all the way down. The boyish figure that lay so still in the very middle of the bed with the blanket tucked in on both sides of him and pulled up under his chin stirred and opened his eyes. When he grimaced and squirmed and finally managed to free his right arm and bring his hand up and gingerly touched his right temple through the turban-like bandage that was wound around his closely-cropped red head, someone who was sitting at his bedside bent over him, gently took his hand and brought it down again. It was Kate McEntee.

"You shouldn't do that, Denny," she told him. "Touching it might start it bleeding again. Does it hurt very much?"

"Some."

"You made a face when you opened your eyes. Does it feel better when your eyes are closed?"

"Uh-huh."

"Then close them and keep them closed."

Someone else came tiptoeing into the room and asked in a low voice:

"Hasn't come to yet, huh?"

Kate nodded and putting her finger against her lips said: "Shh. I think he's gone back to sleep."

Denny felt the closeness of the newcomer as the latter bent over him. He opened his eyes and found Jake Long peering into his face. The lanky puncher grinned at him and asked:

"How you doin', boy?"

"Ohh, all right."

"Good thing for you you've got such a hard head," Jake told him. "Or instead o' that bullet glancin' off your head the way it did, it woulda gone straight in and that woulda been the end o' you." Then taking his eyes from Denny, he raised them to Kate. "You, young'un. You haven't had a minute's rest since this happened. So you must be plumb tuckered out. Now why don't you go take a nap? I'll sit with the boy for a spell. What d'you say?"

"I'm all right, Jake," Kate answered. "Really."

Jake jerked his head around and looked down at Denny, grinned a little and said softly: "Son-uva-gun, he's asleep."

EIGHT

It was evening when Denny awoke. The wick in the lamp had been turned down so low that it cast off only a thin circle of light over the bureau and left the rest of the room in shadows, the far corners in darkness. Forgetting, he turned his head a little too suddenly, and promptly grimaced. But he had already noted that it was not Kate who was occupying the chair next to the bed. It was Matt. And standing a little beyond him and backed against the side wall was Pat. Both youths looked anxiously at Denny, who lay back again with his eyes tightly shut. But after a minute or so he opened them again and without moving his head, asked:

"What time is it?"

"Oh, somewhere's around eight," Matt told him.

"Eight, huh?" Denny repeated. "Slept the whole day away."

"Best thing you coulda done," Pat said. "How d'you feel?"

"Long's I don't forget an' I don't move my head too sudden-like, I'm all right," Denny replied. "You fellers do this, tote me in here an' get me into bed?"

"Uh-huh," Matt said.

"And I owe you for something else," Denny continued. "If you two hadn'ta come bustin' out when you did an' helped me out, while I prob'bly woulda got one o' those fellers comin' up the stairs, chances are the others with him woulda got me. So I'm obliged to you again."

"Way we see it, Denny, we're about even," Pat said. "We'da been in a heckuva fix without you and your buffalo gun."

"Yeah. How'd we do against those raiders?"

"Between the lot of us, the boys in the bunkhouse, Dibbs, Ames, you an' us, we got six o' th'm," Matt told him. "Jake Long says a couple o' th'm were Green's hands and the rest o' th'm musta been chipped in by some o' those other two-bit outfits that don't run any more than say three or four-man crews."

"Six outta how many?" Denny wanted to know.

"Jake isn't sure. But he thinks there were about a dozen in that last bunch that hit us."

"Uh-huh. Now what about your Pa? You buried him, didn't you?"

"Yeah, sure, we buried Pop wrapped up in canvas. 'Course soon's we can, we'll get us a regular coffin and do it right."

"I liked your Pa. He was a good man," Denny said. "I'm sorry I couldn'ta been there when you buried him."

"We know that," Matt said, nodding. "It wasn't much of a service that we gave him. Kate read a piece outta the Bible while Pat, Jake an' me stood by. Dibbs came up here

71

and sat with you while we were takin' care o' Pop."

Denny was silent for a minute or so, then he suddenly asked:

"Think I could get something to eat? My belly's so empty, it's . . . it's growling at me."

Matt grinned and said:

"I know. I heard it." Turning to Pat, he said: "Pat, you wanna give Kate a holler an' tell her ol' blood an' thunder just woke up and that he's plumb starved out?"

"Ol' blood an' thunder, huh?" Pat repeated, grinned and went striding out of the room.

Presently Pat, still grinning, returned, saying as he re-entered the room: "Comin' up, Denny." He sauntered around the bed, and as before, leaned back against the side wall. Minutes later, Kate, carrying a well-laden, towel-covered tray of dishes, appeared in the doorway.

"If you boys will help Denny sit up," Kate said, advancing and setting down the tray on the bed, "one of you on each side of him . . . "

The two youths, followed Kate's instructions, carefully and gently helped Denny up into a sitting position, and held him upright long enough for Kate to square his pillows behind him. He had shut his eyes tightly during the process; now he opened them again.

"All right?" Kate asked him.

"Yeah, fine," he replied. "Only how long do I hafta stay put here? In bed, I mean."

"Till I think you're able to get up," she told him. "For your information, Denny, that bullet dug an inch-long furrow in your temple and left raw, tender flesh that will take time to heal. Then too, it chipped out a piece, a tiny thing of course, of the bone. You'll probably have quite a scar there for the rest of your life." She laid the tray across his thighs, removed the towel, and bending over him, tucked it in under his chin. "I've cut up the meat for you and buttered the biscuits. Want to try and feed yourself?"

"Yeah, sure."

"See you later, Denny," Matt said as he headed for the door.

"Me, too," Pat said, and as he followed his brother, he said over his shoulder: "G'wan, stuff yourself. By the time

72

you feel up to haulin' yourself up outta bed, you'll probably be too doggoned fat to do it by yourself. We'll have to lift you out."

He winked at his sister, and went out.

"They're all right, y'know?" Denny said to Kate. "But you are too." He paused briefly. Then he went on with: "Two things I'm sorry about, though. One's your Pa. He was a good man, and I liked him. Other one's me, for being such a disappointment to you. I'm sorry about that, Kate."

"Don't let your supper get cold," she said, motioning for him to eat. "If it will make you feel better, you haven't been such a disappointment to me. I've begun to think that Pat was right when he said things over which you've had no control have happened, leaving you no alternative but to take a hand in them."

He made no response as he fed himself. She sat back in the chair and watched him.

Finally, he finished, put down the fork and sat back. He met her eyes, smiled and said: "That was good."

"Want to wait a few minutes before you have your coffee?"

"Yeah."

He eased himself back.

"When I'm up and around again," he announced shortly but without looking at her, "I'm pullin' outta here."

"We'll talk about that later on," she answered evenly. "You've a ways to go yet before that."

Minutes later she brought him his coffee together with a generous serving of cake. When he had eaten the last bit of it and drained his cup, she arose, removed the tray and put it on the chair, and made him sit up while she leveled his pillows. Then she eased him down on the flat of his back.

"Stretch out," she instructed him, turned and picked up the tray. "Close your eyes if you like. I'll be back a little later on."

"Thanks, Kate."

She left the room. Half an hour later when Pat looked in on him Denny was asleep. Just as he was about to back out, Kate came in.

"He's asleep," Pat whispered to her. "Dead to the world."

"Come on," Kate whispered back to him.

Pat tiptoed out after her.

Thin rays of daylight were just beginning to penetrate the blind over the window in Denny's room when he awoke the next morning. He stole a look in the direction of the chair. But there was no one sitting in it. So he lay back quietly. After a while his eyes closed and he dozed off. Movement next to the bed woke him. When he opened his eyes he found himself looking up into Kate's face. She was bending over him.

"H'llo," he said.

"Sleep all right?"

"Like a log. What time's it gettin' to be?"

"It's a little after eleven. How about some breakfast?"

"Any time you say."

They heard the measured beat of oncoming horses' hoofs, heard them swell as they neared the house, then fade out. Presently there were bootsteps on the veranda, followed by a heavy-handed knock on the front door.

"Wonder who that could be?" Kate mused. "Be right back, Denny."

"Take your time. I'm not goin' anywhere."

She went out of the room, stopped on the landing when she heard the door open, turned and slowly retraced her steps and halted again astride the bedroom threshold.

"Yeah?" a voice that they recognized as Pat's asked.

"This here is Marshal Thurlow," an unfamiliar voice said. "He wants to see your father."

Kate and Denny heard someone come from the kitchen, and heard his voice shortly.

"Who is it, Pat?"

It was Matt.

"Sheriff," Pat told him, "and a marshal. Wanna c'mere a minute?"

"Yeah, sure," Matt replied. "What's on your mind, Sheriff?

"Wanna see your father. Tell him we're waiting."

"I'm afraid you can't see him."

"You gonna go tell him or are we gonna hafta go tell him ourselves?" a voice that they now recognized as

74

Smith's demanded. "We haven't got all day. So get a hump on."

"Just a minute," an unfamiliar voice said authoritatively. Kate and Denny assumed it was the marshal's. "Is your father around or isn't he, and if he isn't, where'd he go?"

"If it was up to me," Smith said grumpily, "I'd go round up everybody named McEntee, lock th'm up and let them rot in jail which is where they belong. Just because they've got dough, who the hell do they think they are?"

"Take off your spectacles, you old buzzard," Matt said tauntingly, "and I'll pin something on you that'll put that tin star of yours to shame."

"Take it easy, young feller," the marshal said quickly. "And you, Sheriff, suppose you keep outta this an' let me do the talking?"

"Go ahead an' talk," Smith retorted. "Only I'm the law around here and he'd better show some respect for the law, or I'll take him in."

"The hell you will," Matt said clearly.

"Where's your father?" the marshal asked, obviously of Matt.

"Want me to show you?"

"No. Just tell me where we c'n find him."

"All right. 'Round the back o' the house, say about a hundred feet from it, you'll find two graves with a low fence around th'm. Both have markers over th'm. One o' them reads Mary. That's my mother's. The other one's got my father's name on it. It was just put up yesterday, so you won't have 'ny trouble makin' out Matt McEntee."

There was a moment-long silence that even the disgruntled sheriff respected. Then the marshal asked:

"What happened to him?"

"Some o' Milt Green's gunnies came after him when he was headin' home from town. They shot him."

"Milt Green, huh? He's one o' those I laid down the law to this morning."

"His outfit raided us twice last night," Matt related. "First time there were only three of four o' th'm. We got three o' th'm. One was his foreman. Then later on they hit us again. There were eleven o' th'm that came after us that time. We gave it to them good. We got six o' th'm."

No one spoke for a moment.

Then the marshal said "Wanted your father to know this fool range war is over."

"That's nice," Matt commented sarcastically. "Wanna go tell him? I'm sure he'll be glad to hear it."

There was another brief silence. Again it was the marshal who broke it. Apparently turning to the sheriff, he asked:

"What was the name o' the one we came out here to take back with us?"

"Dunno for sure," Smith replied. "Sounded like McCune. I wouldn't swear to it though. But I'd know him in a minute. Snotty redheaded young feller with an itchy trigger finger. A real killer, that one. Told you about him, Marshal. He's the one McEntee put up to killing that Marv Horton and . . ."

"You're a goddamned liar!" Matt, obviously suddenly enraged, yelled at him. "My father never put up anybody to do anything. Now you get the hell outta here, you lyin' old bastid before I . . ."

"I'm takin' you in for makin' threats to the law," Smith said calmly. "You an' that redheaded killer. Marshal . . ."

"Stow it, Smith," the marshal said curtly. Then apparently addressing himself again to Matt: "This McCune or whatever his name is . . . "

"It's McCune," Matt said stiffly.

"What about him? Is he around?"

"Want me to show you where he is?" Matt demanded.

"Y'mean he's dead too?"

"No!" Matt yelled at him. "Green's crew nearly killed him too. Only instead o' the bullet hittin' him square in the head, it glanced off. Half 'n inch the other way and he'da been dead."

"He here?"

"Yeah, he's here."

"Then trot him out," the sheriff ordered.

"Mean you're here to take him in on account o' what this lyin' old bastid's charged him with?" Matt demanded, obviously of the marshal.

"If he's innocent," the latter replied, "he's got nothing to worry about. He doesn't have to prove anything. Up to the law to prove he's guilty. Now where is he?"

"I'll take you to him," Matt said. "Come inside." Apparently Smith started to follow the marshal into the house. "Where are you going, you miserable old bastid?" Matt demanded. He must have blocked the sheriff's way, judging by the brief sounds of scuffling that reached Kate and Denny. "Pat, you stay put here. If he tries to step inside, boot him the hell out. Y'hear?"

"Be a pleasure, Matt," Pat answered. "Just hope he tries to get past me. I'll boot him over the bunkhouse."

"You just wait an' see what happens to you two smart alecks," the angry sheriff sputtered. "I'll be back here with a posse and I'll take both o' you in, lock you up an' throw away the key. Maybe then you'll learn to respect the law."

Pat didn't bother to answer him, while Matt, also ignoring him, said to the marshal: "C'mon." As he led the way to the stairs, he added over his shoulder: "My sister's watchin' over him. If he's asleep, keep your voice down."

There was no response from Thurlow. He followed Matt up the stairs and turned after him when Matt led him down the landing to where Kate was still standing in the open doorway to Denny's room.

"Kate," Matt said as Thurlow and he halted in front of her. "This is Marshal Thurlow. He's here to see Denny. He asleep?"

"No," Kate answered. "He's awake."

She gave the marshal a perfunctory nod, and he took off his hat and murmured: "Ma'am." When she stepped back, turned and walked inside, Matt motioned to Thurlow to follow her, and trooped in at the marshal's heels. Kate had halted at the foot of the bed. Thurlow stopped at the side of it and looked at Denny, then at the bandage around his head.

"Your name McCune?" the marshal asked him.

"Yes, sir. Denny McCune."

Thurlow frowned.

"Way the sheriff told me about you, I expected to find you full growed. But you don't look like more'n a sprout to me. How old are you, boy?"

"Sixteen. Be seventeen next May."

"Sure you aren't older, say like eighteen or nineteen?"

"No, sir."

"He's our cousin," Kate said evenly despite the twin patches of crimson that suddenly burned in her cheeks, a sign of mounting anger within her. "You asked him and he told you. He wouldn't lie to you or to anyone else."

"Only doin' my job, Miss," Thurlow said without looking at her. "Now tell me about this man Horton, Marv Horton. Sheriff claims you shot him down in cold blood. What about it?"

"How's he know?" Denny countered. "He wasn't there when it happened."

"Oh?" the marshal said and he looked surprised.

"That's right," Matt said, and Thurlow turned his gaze on him. "Pop, that is, my father, my brother Pat an' me, and three of our hands who were loading the wagon with stuff we'd bought from Eli Starr who runs the general store, were there. It was my father who told Pat to go get the sheriff and bring him up to where Horton was layin' in an alley right across the street from Starr's place. He wanted the sheriff to know about it right off and from us, instead o' him having to hear about it from somebody else."

"Uh-huh. Suppose you tell me exactly what happened," the marshal said, turning again to Denny.

Quietly and without embellishing his story in any way, Denny told him about the shooting of Marv Horton. Thurlow listened attentively, without once interrupting him or taking his eyes off him, and when the boy had finished his recital, the marshal made no comment but turned and looked at Matt.

"Anything you wanna add to that or change?" he asked.

Matt shook his head and said: "Nope."

"Then far's you c'n remember, that's the way it happened?"

"Wasn't so long ago that I coulda forgotten any of it," Matt answered. "Way Denny just told you is exactly the way it happened."

"Uh-huh," Thurlow said again.

"Coupla things you oughta know, Marshal," Matt said. "To sorta give you an idea of what was going on before this range war started."

"I'm listening," Thurlow said.

"Smith was a storekeeper. A pretty lousy one though. He couldn't make a go of it. That's why, when Joe Watson, who'd been sheriff here for about fifteen years, upped an' died, even before he was buried, Smith went after his job.

78

What the job meant to him, or musta meant to him, was that it would give him a place to live for free an' on top o' that it paid regular wages. I don't think he even gave a thought to what being a lawman would mean. So the way we see it, he's still a storekeeper at heart, only now he's the law around here and he wears a badge, a star, to prove it. But he isn't the . . . the lawman type and he never will be."

"Anything else you think I oughta know?"

"Coming to it. Smith, Green an' Horton were friends from a way back. So it figured he would side in with his friends and that's what he did, against us and the other cattlemen like Lombard, Hill and Parker. So right from the beginning we were in the wrong while Green, Horton and those other two-bit outfits were in the right. Way I've always understood it, the law isn't supposed to take sides with anybody. It's supposed to be neutral, isn't it?"

"That's right," the marshal agreed.

"There's one thing more you might have mentioned, Matt," Kate said, and this time Thurlow faced her squarely. "Even though we've been raided so many times, our cattle's been run off and our men have been shot, we've never retaliated. We've never carried the fighting to anyone beyond our property lines. I think that you should take that into consideration too, Marshal."

"Don't have to, Miss," the marshal replied. "You people aren't being charged with anything. He is though," and he indicated Denny with a nod.

"But it's still that . . . that sheriff's words against so many others," Kate insisted. "He wasn't there when it happened. Yet what he claims seems to be all that matters. Why should that be?"

Thurlow rubbed his nose with the back of his hand.

"I came out here to take him in," he said shortly, again nodding in Denny's direction. "I'm not gonna do that. Judge Leggett will be in town next week, and being that the sheriff is recognized as the law around here, and being that he's the one who's brought the charge against the boy, this young feller will have to come up before the judge, who'll decide whether to put him on trial or let him go."

"That's nice," Matt said. "If the judge goes for what Smith says and doesn't go for what Denny or any of us has to say, Denny'll stand a good chance o' goin' to prison. Right?"

"Don't go gettin' ahead o' yourself," the marshal said, turning back to Matt. "Judge Leggett's been around a long time, and while he c'n be as hard as nails when there's a call for it, he isn't the kind to be, we-ll, taken in by anybody. Boy'll get a fair shake from him. You c'n depend on that. Now look, I'm leavin' the boy here, only I'm makin' you people responsible for him. When the judge is ready to see him, I'll come out here for him, and you people c'n come along too so's you c'n be on hand if the judge wants to hear from you. All right?"

Neither Kate nor Matt answered. Thurlow clapped on his hat, then lifted it and put it on again, settling it more securely on his head. When he turned to go, Matt, grim-faced, led the way out of the room, down the landing and down the stairs. Pat, who was squarely in the middle of the open front doorway, turned his head and looked at them as they came toward him. Smith, standing outside on the veranda, peered in at Matt, at the marshal and then past the lawman. He looked wide-eyed with surprise, and pushing his spectacles higher up on his nose, asked:

"Where is he?"

"Let's go," Thurlow said curtly.

"Where's that redheaded kid?" the sheriff asked him.

"In bed, shot up," the marshal answered.

"Shoulda hauled him up outta there anyway so's we coulda taken him in with us. This way it'll mean makin' another ride out here to get him and . . . "

"When we need him, I'll come for him."

"And who's gonna be held responsible if he's hightailed it before then?"

"You won't be," Thurlow retorted, evidence that he was out of patience with him. "I will. Meantime though, Mister, I'm gonna give you a tip. If I were you, just to be on the safe side, kinda think I'd start lookin' around for another job. Something that's more in your line. C'mon. Let's go."

NINE

Kate and Denny heard the front door close, heard the thump of booted feet as Thurlow and Smith crossed the veranda to their waiting horses. A moment or so later they heard the swift drum of hoofs as the two lawmen rode away. The hoofbeats swelled briefly, then they faded away. From below came the indistinct murmur of the McEntee boys' voices. Kate, still angry-looking and still a little flushed, glanced at Denny. He sat head bowed, staring down at his clasped hands. She perched herself on the edge of the bed, leaned toward him, and cupping his chin in her right hand, forced him to raise his head and meet her eyes.

"Look," she said severely. "You haven't yet appeared before that judge. So don't let your imagination run away with you, and don't go picturing yourself in prison."

His eyes fell before hers.

"Look at me," she commanded. "I haven't finished with you." Reluctantly he raised his eyes. "Now then, let's get one thing understood before you tell me again, as you have so many times already, that you shouldn't have come here. You came here because this is where you belong. My father told you you were part of the family, didn't he? So I don't want ever again to hear you say that, or that you should have gone off on your own, or that when you're up and around again you're going to leave us, or anything else as silly as all that. While you're still a McCune and always will be, to all intents and purposes you're a McEntee, and McEntees never give up without putting up a fight. Remember that, Denny. Because you're one of us, this isn't just your fight. It's ours too. So do as we'll be doing. Preparing to fight."

Matt and Pat came striding into the room.

"Kate," Matt began briskly and without any preliminaries. "I think we oughta have a lawyer to do the talking for Denny."

"I think so too," Pat said. "D'you remember the name o' that lawyer Pop had over at Medina?"

"I think it was Wicker," Kate said.

"Pop liked him," Matt said. "I don't remember his

name. Only that Pop said he was smart an' sharp as all get-out."

"Mark Wicker," Kate told him.

"Gonna send for him," Matt said. "If this Judge Leggett looks like he's goin' for what that . . . that lyin' Smith tells him, I think it'll be a good idea to have somebody smart to talk up for Denny. If this Wicker feller is so good, he oughta be able to make a monkey outta Smith, and show the judge that he's believing the wrong one."

"Send for him," Kate said. "By all means. But don't lose any time. There's no telling how soon that marshal will be back here for Denny."

"Gonna 'tend to it right away," Matt assured her. "I'm goin' right down to the bunkhouse and tell Jake Long to saddle up and ride into town and send Wicker a telegram to come a-running."

Matt went hustling out of the room and down the landing, down the stairs and out the front door. They heard it close and latch after him.

"Now, young feller," Pat said, turning to Denny. "All you've gotta do is get yourself strong enough to stand up on your own two feet for when that marshal comes to take you before the judge. Far's I c'n see, you haven't got anything to worry about. You'll be in Wicker's hands, and you couldn't ask for better."

Two days later, much to the McEntees' dismay, the marshal made an unexpected reappearance. It was Kate who came hurrying out from the kitchen in response to his knock on the front door. The moment she opened it and saw him standing on the other side of the threshold strip, she paled and exclaimed:

"Oh, no!"

Gravely he said: "Sorry, Ma'am. But like I told you the last time, I'm only doin' my job."

"I know," she admitted unhappily. "We had hoped you wouldn't be back till our lawyer got here."

"Tell you the truth, Ma'am, I didn't expect to be back here so soon either. Y'see, Judge Leggett took sick in Ashford and now he's laid up there in his hotel room with a doctor takin' care o' him. So another judge, man named

82

Roland, is fillin' in for him. Soon's Roland got word, he headed for Ludlow fast as he could. Got in late yesterday afternoon. While I was away. Soon's he got here, the sheriff got his ear. Minute I got back, Roland sent for me and told me to go get the boy. So like it or not, Ma'am, here I am. How's the boy doin'?"

"He's feeling better. Still weak though."

"He dressed?"

"Yes. Sitting at the window in his room soaking in some of the sunshine. I don't think it would be advisable for him to try to ride his horse into town with you, Marshal. I'm afraid the jouncing would be too much for him."

"Got a rig we c'n use?"

"Yes. Behind the barn."

"Well, suppose you go get one o' your hands to hitch up the rig? Meanwhile, if it's all right with you, I'll go up and let the boy know I'm here."

"Of course, Marshal. You know the way, don't you?"

"I think so. Turn right when I come off the stairs. Last room on the floor."

She nodded. She was about to open the door wider to permit the marshal to enter when she checked herself and asked:

"Marshal, this Judge Roland. What kind of a person is he?"

"Never had 'ny dealings with him before this, Ma'am. So I don't think I c'n say for sure one way or another. All I c'n tell you about him is what I've heard said. He isn't another Leggett. They don't make Leggett's kind in bunches, not even in two's. Now don't get me wrong. I've never heard anything against this Roland. All I've heard said is that he's fair to most who come up before him."

"I hope he'll be fair to Denny," Kate said fervently.

She moved with the door, held it wide open for him. Still holding the door and following him with her eyes, Kate saw him top the stairs, turn and start down the landing. Slowly, with her expression one of deep concern, she went out. She was about midway between the house and the barn when three mounted men whom she recognized at once came loping into view, cutting between the bunkhouse and the corral. She beckoned vigorously, and cupping her hands around her mouth cried: "Matt!" He looked up instantly,

83

and when she beckoned a second time, he said something to the two who were with him, Pat and lanky Jake Long. When he quickened his horse's pace, they dashed after him. They came up to Kate shortly and brought their horses to a sliding, dust-raising stop in front of her. She had to turn her head to protect her eyes from the dust.

"S'matter, Sis?" Matt wanted to know.

Turning back to him, she nodded in the direction of the house and the three looked there too.

"Whose horse is that standing there?" Matt asked her.

"The marshal's," she replied. "He's come for Denny."

"Y'mean that Judge Leggett's hit town already? Thought Thurlow said it wouldn't be till next week?"

"It isn't Judge Leggett," Kate explained. "He's ill. So another man, a Judge Roland, is here instead. The marshal couldn't tell me very much about him. Only that he's said to be fair with most who come up before him. What worries me is how fair will he be with Denny? Oh, I wish Mark Wicker had come!"

Matt McEntee swung down from his horse. Pat dismounted too.

"I told the marshal I didn't think it would be advisable for Denny to ride his horse to town, that the jouncing might be too much for him in view of his weakened condition," Kate continued. "Will one of you have the rig hitched up? Denny should find riding in that lots more comfortable."

Matt passed his reins to Jake.

"Jake," he said tightening his belt. "Be a good feller and tell Lee Dibbs to hitch up the rig and drive it up to the house. Where's Thurlow now, Kate?"

"Upstairs with Denny."

"Uh-huh. C'mon, Pat."

The latter half-turned to Long and held out the reins to him.

"Take my horse along too, will you, Jake?"

"Sure," the puncher replied, taking the reins from Pat. Then addressing himself to Matt, he asked: "How about me driving the rig to town? The more friends the boy sees around him, the better he'll feel."

"Good idea, Jake," Matt said. Then he added: "Being that Pat an' me'll be going along to town, don't put our horses inside. Leave th'm outside in front o' the barn."

Long nodded and wheeled away and led the youths' horses down to the barn. With Matt on one side of her and Pat on the other, Kate led the way up to the house. As they neared it, they saw two figures emerge from it. One was Denny. His head was still heavily bandaged. The other was Thurlow, who towered over him. At the marshal's instance, Denny crossed the veranda and eased himself down on the top step. Thurlow sauntered forward and stood next to him with his big hands on his hips. After a moment his hands moved. He hooked his thumbs in his gunbelt. As the three McEntees came up the path to the steps, the marshal nodded a greeting and said:

"We're ready to go soon's that rig o' yours shows up."

"It'll be along directly," Matt answered. He stopped in front of Denny, peered at him and asked: "How you doin'?"

"All right."

"Jake's gonna drive you an' Kate. Pat an' me'll be right behind you."

Denny withheld his reply for a moment. Then he said:

"I know you fellers have a lot o' things to 'tend to. So I hate to take you away from th'm. Wouldn't it do for just Jake to go with me?"

"Nope, wouldn't do at all," Matt said firmly.

There were hoofbeats beyond them from the direction of the barn, and the McEntees turned and watched Jake Long come toward the house in the rig while the boys' horses, their reins tied to the tailgate, trotted along behind it. Presently Jake pulled up in front of the house. Thurlow bent and helped Denny to his feet. He followed with Denny when Kate and her brothers retraced their steps down the path to the waiting rig. Kate was helped into it. She moved to the far end of the seat, leaving room for Denny between Jake and herself. With Long reaching down and giving Denny a hand up and the marshal practically boosting him up from the rear, and Kate, with her hands on his hips, guiding him backward into his seat, Denny was soon comfortably settled. Thurlow turned and walked back to his waiting horse and swung himself up into the saddle. Matt and Pat untied their horses and climbed up on them. Long squared back on the seat and asked:

"What d'you say, young feller? All set?"

"Yeah, sure," Denny answered. "All set."

The rig wheeled away from the house. Denny turned in his seat and looked back at it.

"It's a swell house, y'know?" he said, and because there was a trace of sadness in his voice, both Kate and Long looked at him. "Nice an' big an' comf'table."

"And you're coming back to it," she assured him.

The marshal, he noticed, had already pulled into position alongside the rig; a backward glance revealed the presence of Matt and Pat directly behind it. As they came abreast of the barn, Dibbs and Ames, who were standing in the open doorway with the latter cradling a rifle in his arms despite his awareness that the range war was over and that there would be no more raids, called a cheery "Good luck, young feller." Denny acknowledged with a little wave of his hand. A minute later they passed through the arched entrance to the McEntee place with the signboard bearing the 'McE' squarely overhead, slowed a bit when they came to the open road, wheeled and headed for Ludlow and Denny's appearance before Judge Roland.

Proof that the range war was over and that the law in the formidable personage of Thurlow and the other marshals had the situation well in hand was the activity and the presence of many people in Ludlow's main street. The stores were open and appeared to be thronged with customers. There were buckboards and wagons huddling close to the low and uneven wooden curb on both sides of the street, while the hitchrails, which seemed to be everywhere, looked to be crowded to capacity with tied-up horses. Passersby, most of them women with marketing baskets swinging from their hands, were standing about in little groups and talking among themselves. They looked up interestedly when the Thurlow-led party came up the street. When the rig swerved and cut in toward the curb and finally pulled up in front of the sheriff's office, the townspeople began to converge upon the spot from all directions. A tall, rangy man, who was built like Thurlow and who was standing a little spread-legged with his hands on his hips and backed against Smith's window, straightened up as Thurlow dismounted and then came out to the curb to meet him. The badge he wore pinned to the pocket of his shirt was identical with Thurlow's; he wore his gun low slung and tied down around his right thigh just as Thurlow did. The latter looped his reins around the hitchrail, nodded to the other man, stepped up on the walk, came to Kate's side and helped her get down.

"All right, young feller," he said to Denny who had already begun to move across the seat toward the marshal. "Easy now."

As Denny climbed down and stood waiting, the second marshal came up behind Thurlow and asked in a low voice:

"That the kid the sheriff's been makin' such a to-do about?"

"Uh-huh."

"Heck, he's only a sprout. I've seen a lot o' killers in my time. But never any that looked like this kid."

"Can't always go by looks, Bill. Same time, though, I wouldn't go by what that sheriff says."

"That Smith's a pretty sorry lookin' kind of a lawman, isn't he?"

"The sorriest," Thurlow replied over his shoulder. "For my dough he's still what he was before he took to wearin' a star."

"Storekeeper, I think you said. Right, Tom?"

"Right. C'mon, boy," Thurlow said to Denny. He took him by the arm and turned to lead him into the office. Then he stopped abruptly and looked back and shook his head at the McEntees and Jake Long, who were following him, and they stopped too and lifted questioning eyes to him. "Think you folks'd better wait out here for now. I'll tell the judge you're here. When he says he wants to see you, I'll let you know."

"C'mon over here with me," Bill suggested to them.

A little reluctantly, after casting a disappointed and apprehensive look in Denny's direction, they trooped after Bill to where he had been standing earlier. Thurlow glanced over the swelling number of townspeople that had begun to crowd the narrow walk, and frowned. He shook his head, turned and opened the office door and ushered Denny inside ahead of him. There was a desk directly ahead of him, and behind it sat a man with an unruly mop of white hair and gold rimmed spectacles that kept slipping down the length of his nose, forcing him to push them up again. The man behind the desk looked up, squared back in his chair, looked hard at Denny, then past him and said:

"Thank you, Marshal. Will you wait outside, please?"

"Yeah, sure, Judge. Just wanted to tell you that the boy's people are here in case you wanna see them."

The judge nodded and again said: "Thank you."

Denny heard the door open behind him and close again. He had already glimpsed the sheriff standing off to a side. But he did not look at him. He kept his eyes fixed on the judge.

"All right, son," the latter began. "Give me your full name. Incidentally, what happened to your head?"

"The McEntees musta put him up to wearin' the bandage, Judge," the sheriff said. "You know, to get him some sympathy. For my dough that bandage is an out-an'-out fake. Want me to take it off so's you c'n see for yourself?"

"No," Roland said bluntly. Then he retorted: "If there isn't anything wrong with his head, why is there blood on the bandage, and fresh blood at that? If you don't mind, Sheriff, I'll conduct this hearing by myself and without any assistance from you." He looked up at Denny. "What happened to your head, son?"

"Got nicked on the temple by a bullet. Gouged out a tiny hunk o' bone and a lotta flesh. Wound's still kinda raw. So it bleeds on an' off. 'Specially when I move my head too sudden-like."

"Have you had a doctor look at it?"

"Haven't got a doctor 'round these parts."

The judge frowned. Then he said:

"State your name."

"Denny McCune."

Roland noted it on a blank sheet of paper in front of him.

"Age?" he asked.

"Sixteen. Be seventeen next May."

The sheriff scoffed openly and the judge shot a look at him.

"He's a liar, Judge. He's eighteen or nineteen if he's a day."

"Sheriff," Roland said quietly. "Either keep your opinions and your comments to yourself, or I shall have to ask you to wait outside with the marshal."

"Sorry," Smith said, pushing his spectacles up on his nose. Unconsciously the judge did the same thing with his spectacles.

"Sixteen," the judge repeated, and wrote it down on the paper below Denny's name. Again he raised his eyes. "I don't know if you understand this, Denny. This isn't a trial. It is a hearing. The purpose of it is to give me an opportunity to examine you and decide whether to dismiss the charge that has been brought against you and discharge you . . . let you go . . . or order you to stand trial. Do you understand that, Denny?"

"Yes, sir."

"Good," Roland said nodding. "Do you know the nature of the charge against you?"

"Yes, sir. I killed a man named Horton. Marv Horton. Sheriff says I murdered him."

"Did you murder him?"

"No, sir."

"Tell me briefly what happened."

"I saw this man, this Marv Horton, hidin' in an alley with his rifle raised, fixin' to shoot Mr. McEntee. I let out a holler to warn Mr. McEntee, and fired before this Marv Horton could shoot."

"Aside from you and Mr. McEntee, who else was there at the time of the shooting?"

"The McEntee boys, Matt an' Pat, and three o' the McEntee hands. The hands were loading up a wagon with all kinds o' stuff from the general store."

"Were there any others aside from those whom you have mentioned, outsiders, I mean, present who might have witnessed the affair?"

"No, sir," Denny replied. "Leastways, nobody that I know of, or heard tell of."

"Was the sheriff there?"

"No, sir. He was in his office. Mr. McEntee sent Pat to fetch him."

"To repeat, Denny, to the best of your knowledge, do you know of anyone at all who might have witnessed the shooting?"

"No, sir."

"Then I must tell you that there is someone who claims she witnessed the entire affair. She is ready to appear in court and is prepared to swear that it was not as you have described it, but a cold-blooded murder." When there was no response from Denny, Judge Roland continued with: "In view of that, Denny McCune, I have no alternative but to order you to stand trial at which time you may be represented by counsel . . . a lawyer, that is. Sheriff . . ."

"Yes, sir, Judge?"

"Please have Marshal Thurlow bring in the eldest member of the defendant's family."

Denny moved aside to permit Smith to reach the door. When the sheriff came abreast of him, he gave Denny a scornful little smile, opened the door and went out. Denny stood motionless.

"In view of your extreme youth, Denny," Roland said, "I am going to release you on bond. When a date for trial has been set, you will be informed of it."

Denny made no response.

"I'm sorry, son," the judge added. "But I have no alternative but to do as the law prescribes. Until you are brought to trial, you are not to leave the limits of this county. If you do, the bond will be forfeited, and when you are apprehended . . . caught . . . you will be turned over to the sheriff and confined here till the time for your appearance in court. Do you understand that?"

Before Denny could answer, the door opened and the sheriff returned, followed by Matt McEntee and Marshal Thurlow. The latter closed the door and stood with his back to it and his thumbs hooked in his gunbelt. Smith moved to the front of the desk and bent over it and whispered to the judge who listened and nodded. When the sheriff finished, Roland waved him away. Smith sauntered off to where he had been standing but minutes before, halted there and turned around. Raising his eyes to Matt, the judge said:

"I had heard of your late father. However, I had never had the pleasure of meeting him. I am sorry to hear of his death." When there was no response from Matt, Roland continued with: "I am willing to release the defendant in your custody. Are you prepared to post a bond guarantee-

90

ing his appearance in court upon the date to be set for trial?"

"Just tell me how much and I'll go an' get it."

"Five hundred dollars."

"Gimme five minutes and I'll be back with it."

Roland smiled and said:

"Of course."

Matt turned on his heel and headed for the door. Thurlow opened it and closed it after him. Then the marshal came forward to the desk.

"Got something I'd like to discuss with you in private, Judge," he said with a meaningful glance in the sheriff's direction.

"Very well, Marshal. Sheriff, will you excuse us, please?"

Smith was annoyed, and his expression reflected his feelings.

"Bein' that I'm the law around here an' that this is my office that you're puttin' me out've, I think I oughta have the right to hear what he's gotta say."

Roland looked at Thurlow who said:

"Might be just as well, I guess, to let him stay and hear it."

"Just as you say, Marshal."

"I've been doin' a lot o' nosing around an' talkin' to a lot o' people these last two days, and I wanna tell you what I've come up with," Thurlow began. "First off, the town council that's made up o' three people, and all o' th'm are storekeepers, are the ones who gave Smith the sheriff's job. Only one o' th'm thought Smith was doin' a pretty fair job. The other two voted to let him, Smith that is, have the job because they had to have somebody in a helluva . . . excuse me, Judge . . . heckuva sweat and because there wasn't anybody else around who was willing to take it. He isn't a lawman, Judge. You oughta be able to see that for yourself. He was a storekeeper before he pinned on the star and he still is."

Smith was bristling. But he held his tongue.

"Smith and Matt McEntee, the father o' that young feller who was just in here . . . "

"Judge knows all about th'm," the sheriff said, interrupting him. "From me. Same's he knows that they put that

91

young feller up to killin' Marv Horton."

The marshal squared around to him.

"That's a lie, Smith, and you know it, and any time you think you're man enough to make me eat what I've just called you, lemme know." Thurlow turned away from him. "Like I was gonna say, Judge, Smith and Matt McEntee didn't get along. So Smith's takin' it out on the boy," and he waved his hand in Denny's direction. "Smith an' that Marv Horton were old friends. So goin' by what I've picked up here an' there, I think Smith figgered that by framin' the boy and chargin' him with murder he'd be gettin hunk with McEntee and at the same time get revenge for Horton's gettin' himself shot."

"Don't you believe him, Judge!" Smith cried out.

Roland ignored him.

"You'll get your chance in court, Marshal, to repeat what you've just said, just as the sheriff will be given an opportunity to defend himself."

"What's the date for the trial?" Thurlow asked.

"I think we'll set it for a week from today."

Thurlow nodded, turned on his heel and headed for the door. He gave Denny a reassuring wink as he left the office.

TEN

Thurlow and Bill were standing together a little apart from Kate, Pat and Jake Long when Denny and Matt emerged from the sheriff's office. The crowd of curious townspeople surged forward but stopped when the two marshals, moving alertly ahead of the McEntees, forced the crowd to back up; then they opened a path to the curb. There was some shoving and pushing among the onlookers and here and there some angry words were exchanged between those who were trampled and those who did the trampling. Thurlow and Bill stood silently looking on as Jake helped Kate and then Denny mount the high step and climb up to the wide seat. Thurlow and Bill stood silently looking on as Jake helped Kate and then Denny mount the high step and climb up to the wide seat. Thurlow shifted his gaze to the McEntee youths and watched them hoist themselves up on their horses. When the rig wheeled around and started

92

downstreet with Matt and Pat loping along behind it, the crowd began to disperse. As before, passersby stopped and looked up as the rig neared them and then came abreast of them; they followed it with their eyes as it rumbled on, reached the corner and took the road west.

Ludlow had long since dropped away behind, when Matt ranged up alongside of the rig and Kate turned questioning eyes upon him.

"If we don't hear 'nything from that Wicker character by tomorrow morning," he told her grimly, "I think we'd better do something about gettin' us another lawyer."

"How much time do we have before the trial?"

"Week," Matt replied.

"I think we ought to wait a while longer than just one day. The fact that we haven't heard from Mr. Wicker may simply mean that he's away. I'm sure we'll hear something from him the moment he returns. I'm quite certain he won't ignore your message."

"All right," Matt conceded. "So we'll wait a mite longer. I know he's a good lawyer, probably the best around, and we want the best we c'n get for Denny. Just hope we hear he's on his way. I'll feel a lot better then about things."

"So will I."

He slowed his horse and permitted the rig to get ahead of him and resumed his place at Pat's side. After that, there was no more conversation among any of them. The unhurried pace that the rig maintained made the trip far longer than it would have normally been. Kate glanced at Denny a couple of times; once when he must have felt her eyes on him, he looked at her. She didn't say anything. Instead she simply smiled, reached over and squeezed his hand, her way of reassuring him. From time to time, Jake too looked at him, and when Denny met his eyes, the lanky man reached over with his big, bony hand and patted Denny on the knee. They were about a mile from home when Kate happened to steal another look at Denny. His eyes were closed and his head was bowed and nodding. She bent quickly and peered up at him. Jake looked at her.

"S'matter?" he asked.

"Shh," she answered in a guarded tone. "He's asleep."

"Trip musta knocked him out, huh?"

"Too much for him in his weakened condition."

"Poor kid," Jake said and promptly slowed his team to an unhurried walk.

Carefully, so as to avoid waking him, Kate, half-turning to Denny, reached out and curled her left arm around the boy and brought his nodding head to rest on her shoulder.

When the rig neared the barn, Dibbs and Ames appeared in the doorway, the latter without his rifle this time. Dibbs came hurrying down the ramp as the rig pulled up in front of him. He pointed in the direction of the house, and all eyes followed his finger. Standing in front of the house was a buckboard with a hoof-pawing and obviously impatient horse in its shafts.

"Belongs to a feller named Wicker," Dibbs said. "He's a lawyer and told me you folks'd sent for him."

"There you are, Matt," Kate said happily to her elder brother.

"I'm doggoned glad he got here," Matt said. "Where is he, Lee? Inside?"

"Uh-huh," the puncher replied. "Didn't know how long you folks'd be gone, and I didn't think you'd want him to wait in the buckboard till you got back. So I took him inside and turned him over to Ming. Betcha by now that Chinaman's got him so full o' coffee he's about ready to float."

"Thanks, Lee," Kate said. "Jake, I think we'd better go right on up to the house."

"Right," Jake acknowledged, and drove on.

Matt and Pat dismounted and Dibbs led their horses up the ramp and into the barn. When the two youths entered the house through the front door, they heard voices coming from the kitchen, and they headed for it. There was no sign of Denny. But Kate was there. She was sitting at the table, leaning over her folded arms and talking earnestly with a pleasant-faced man of about forty who got to his feet an held out his hand, first to Matt, then to Pat. The handshake he gave each of them was strong and reassuring.

"Your sister has just told me about your father," he said to them. "I'm shocked beyond belief. He was a fine, upstanding man, and I regret his untimely passing as deeply as I know you young people must. It was a privilege to handle his legal matters for him, and his repeated expressions of confidence in me were very gratifying. Please

94

accept my deepest sympathies."

He sat down again. As the youths seated themselves at the table, Ming who had just placed a cup of coffee in front of Kate, brought them coffee too. But when he sought to refill Mark Wicker's cup, the lawyer stopped him with a shake of his head.

"Now then," Wicker began. "Your message said you wanted or needed me in a hurry. What's the problem?"

Kate and Matt looked at each other.

"Go ahead, Kate," Matt said. "You c'n tell him."

"It's our cousin, Denny McCune," Kate said, turning again to the lawyer. "He's sixteen. But he goes on trial a week from today charged with murder. That's why we sent for you, Mr. Wicker. To defend him."

Wicker's eyebrows arched.

"Sixteen, eh, and charged with murder? H'm," he said. "Is he guilty?"

"Not of murder," Matt said quickly, before Kate could answer. "But of killing a man who was fixin' to shoot Pop. Denny shot him before he could pull the trigger."

"I see," the lawyer said. "And where is the young man?"

"He's out on bond," Matt said.

"He's upstairs," Kate added. "He's pretty weak from a bullet wound he suffered when we were raided a couple of nights ago. Since he had to appear before Judge Roland this morning . . . "

"I assume that was just a hearing."

"Oh?" Kate said. "We drove into town with Denny. It's fourteen miles, seven each way. It took a lot out of Denny, so much in fact that just before we got here, he dozed off. Anyway, as soon as we got back to the house, I told him to go straight up to his room and to get into bed. You won't mind seeing him upstairs, will you?"

"No, of course not," was the prompt reply.

Kate looked at her brothers.

"Finished with your coffee?" she asked.

"Yep," Pat answered, pushed back from the table and got to his feet.

Matt got up too, but with his cup in his hand, took a last swallow of coffee and put down the cup.

"Let's go," he said.

Moments later, with Kate leading the way and the

lawyer following her, and the two youths trudging along behind them, they trooped up the stairs and marched down the landing to Denny's room. He was sitting up in bed. He looked at Kate. Then his gaze shifted to Mark Wicker and held on him.

"Denny," Kate said. "This is our lawyer, Mr. Wicker. He's going to defend you in court."

"Hello, Denny," Wicker said, stepped up close to the bed, bent a little and held out his hand to the boy who gripped it and released it. "Kate has given me a general idea of what we're up against. Think you're up to giving me some of the details?"

"Yeah, sure."

"Mr. Wicker," Kate said, pointing to the bedside chair.

The lawyer nodded, moved past her and around the bed to the far side of it and seated himself, moved himself and the chair a little closer to the bed, smiled at Denny, and said:

"I'd like to know everything that happened up to the shooting and after. Take your time and don't overtax yourself. Stop and rest whenever you feel the need of it. So whenever you're ready, son . . . "

Matt and Pat had already backed against the near-side wall, while Kate, who had been standing at the foot of the bed, perched herself on the edge of it and pushed back a little till her shoulders nudged the bedpost. Then she sat still, with her clasped hands in her lap. Unhurriedly and simply, just as he had recited his story of the shooting of Marv Horton to Marshal Thurlow, Denny repeated it for Wicker. The latter sat quietly and listened attentively, his gaze holding on Denny throughout. Then just as the marshal had done, the lawyer raised his eyes to Matt.

"Anything you want to correct in Denny's story, or add?"

Matt shook his head.

Wicker's eyes shifted to Pat.

"Anything you want to say?" he asked.

"No, sir. Far as I c'n remember, everything happened just the way Denny said it did."

"Good. Now what happened at the hearing?" Wicker asked, turning again to Denny.

"I'm not supposed to leave the county," the boy replied.

"Oh, seems like there's somebody who says he saw the whole thing and that it wasn't anything like the way I said it was."

"Obviously that's why you're going to stand trial."

Denny made no reply to that.

"Did the judge identify this individual, this witness, for you?"

"No, sir. Judge didn't say who he is and I didn't ask. All I did was answer whatever he asked me. Outside o' that, I didn't say anything on my own. And I didn't ask him anything because I didn't think I shoulda. Figgered you'd do that."

"Of course," Wicker said.

"You going to town?" Matt asked the lawyer.

"As soon as I finish here," the latter replied. "I'll want to see the judge and everyone else who might have an interest in the case. Most of all, though, I hope to find someone who can substantiate Denny's story."

"Uh-huh," Matt said. "When you get to town, might be a good idea for you to look up Marshal Thurlow."

"That his name, or is marshal his title?"

"He's a U. S. marshal. Judgin' by what I heard him say to the sheriff who's the one making all the trouble for Denny, Thurlow doesn't think any more o' the sheriff than we do. I think the marshal'll give it to you straight, whatever you wanna know of him, providin', of course, that he knows. He strikes me as being that kind o' lawman, straight and fair."

Wicker nodded and stood up, half-turned and moved the chair back to its original place, turned again and said:

"In all likelihood I won't be back here today. Tomorrow sometime. But don't get concerned if I fail to return even then. Just take it for granted that I'm working in my client's behalf, and that I'll be back as soon as I can, and I hope, with something worthwhile to report." He gave Denny a smile. "Thank you for your cooperation, Denny."

Kate had already gotten to her feet. The boys straightened up. Wicker started to round the bed.

"Mr. Wicker," Denny said, and the lawyer stopped and leveled a questioning look at him. "Mr. Wicker," Denny said a second time, "there any chance o' me goin' to prison?"

"I don't think so," Wicker answered. "The chance of that happening is a very remote one. After all, you aren't a criminal with a record. You're . . . we-ll, you're just a boy who did what he thought was right, instinctively too, I might add, when he saw someone close to him in danger of being shot down." The lawyer smiled and asked: "You haven't compiled a record like that, have you? And isn't this the first time you've come in conflict with the law?"

"I think you'd better tell Mr. Wicker everything, Denny," Kate said quietly, and the lawyer, who had turned to her, quickly shifted his gaze back to Denny. "It wouldn't be fair to him not to know everything about you."

"The worst thing, the most frustrating thing too, that can happen to a lawyer," Wicker said, "is for him to go into court and hear things about his client that he should have been told long before that but which had been kept from him. By all means, tell me everything. I'll be better equipped to prepare the proper defense for you, and I'll be prepared to cope with anything that might arise."

Denny flashed Kate a reproachful look, a sign that he knew what she was referring to, but that he saw no connection between that and the charge that was pending against him.

"What's that gotta do with this?" he asked her grumpily.

"Why don't you tell me what it is and let me be the judge?" Wicker asked him.

Denny wiped his mouth with the back of his hand, meeting the lawyer's eyes at the same time.

"What Kate means for me to tell you happened before I came here," Denny said. "Where I used to live. In Oklahoma."

Wicker held his tongue. He waited for Denny to continue. Then just as Denny was about to speak, Wicker asked:

"Whereabouts in Oklahoma?"

"Place called Walkersville."

The lawyer nodded and said: "Go on, please."

"My Pa'd been having some trouble with some folks named Lamson. Three brothers, they were. It was on account of a stream that ran b'tween their place and ours. Over who owned it. Court was supposed to decide. Only it hadn't got around to sayin', when Pa was killed. By the Lamsons. Way I see it, they musta got tired o' waitin' so

long to hear and musta decided to settle the thing themselves and in their own way. So they cut down on Pa when
they saw him down near the stream, on our side of it,
watering our horses, and killed him." Slowly, almost
painstakingly, Denny continued with the rest of the story
for Wicker's benefit, and concluded with: "That's it, Mr.
Wicker."

"Sure you haven't omitted anything?"

"I'm sure. What's more, I told it to you just the way it
happened."

"The judge who freed you . . . ?"

"Name's Hawks."

"And the sheriff?"

"Buck Flowers. Big feller. Not a puny one like the
sheriff we've got here."

"Aside from Kate, did you tell your story to anyone
else?"

"To Mr. McEntee. Told him right off. Matt an' Pat were
there and they heard it. Later on I told Kate."

"Tell anyone else?"

"No, sir."

"The marshal or the sheriff?"

"No, sir."

Wicker took his gaze from Denny and looked around at
the others.

"How about you people?" he asked. "Any of you tell it
to anyone?"

There was a general shaking of heads.

"Think your father might have told it to anyone?"

"Pop wasn't the kind to go talkin' outta turn," Matt said.
"So I don't think he woulda told it to anybody."

"Actually it doesn't really matter if anyone else knows
about it," Wicker said. "As long as I know about it too."

"Fact that Judge Hawks let me go," Denny said, and the
lawyer turned to him again, "oughtn't that be good enough
in case somebody's found out about it and it gets brought
up in court?"

"The important thing, Denny, as I just said, is that I
know about it," Wicker said patiently. "So if it should be
brought out in court, I won't be taken by surprise. I'll be
prepared for it and I'll be ready to answer."

"Uh-huh," was Denny's response.

"Now is there anything else in which you were involved? This is the time for you to tell me, y'know. For your information, son, the law says, and quite clearly too, that whatever is confided to either a lawyer or a doctor is inviolate. That means that neither a lawyer nor a doctor can be compelled to reveal a confidence. So if there is anything else you want to confide to me . . . "

"Nope. Nothing else."

Wicker nodded and said: "Good. Hope you'll feel better and that you'll be up and about the next time I see you. Bye, Denny."

He gave each of the boys a smile and a nod and followed Kate out of the room. Denny stared gloomily into space.

"Hey, no call for you to look so blamed down in the mouth," Matt said to him. "You've got a doggoned good man workin' for you, and he don't look half as worried as you do. So c'mon, cheer up."

"What's he got to worry about?" Denny retorted. "No chance o' him havin' to go to prison. Besides, he's gonna get paid for what he's gonna do for me. And that's something that's got me down, maybe even more than anything else." He squared back against his pillow and met Matt's eyes. "How am I ever gonna be able to pay you back for what this Wicker feller is gonna cost you?" Suddenly though, before Matt could answer, a thought came to Denny and he said: "Matt, be a good feller and open the top drawer in the bureau. Poke around in there till you find a small canvas bag. It's prob'ly buried under everything else in there."

"And when I find it?" Matt asked.

"There's twenty-seven bucks in the bag. It isn't such a heckuva lot and I know blamed well it won't make much of a dent in Wicker's bill. But I want it to go toward the bill anyway."

Matt moved away from the wall and halted at the side of the bed and looked hard at the boy who was propped up in it.

"Look," he began. "Instead o' worryin' about dough and bills, supposin' you stick to getting better? Everything else will take care of itself. Pop used to say that things have a way o' workin' themselves out and he was right a heckuva

100

lot more often than he was wrong."

"But . . . "

"I'm not finished yet, bucko. Besides, I'm older'n you. So show some respect for my years and listen, and listen good. We don't want your dough. You're part o' this family. Remember? I keep telling you that but I never know for sure if you believe it. If Pop was around he wouldn't take your dough anymore'n he'd take mine or Pat's or Kate's, and we won't take it either. Pop left us pretty well fixed, and 'us' includes you because I know that's the way he woulda wanted it. So I don't wanna hear 'nymore outta you about dough or bills. Understand?" He gave Denny no opportunity to answer, turned instead to Pat and said: "I kinda think Denny's had enough for a while and c'n use some peace an' quiet. So what d'you say we make ourselves scarce around here and come back later on, huh?"

"I'm waitin' on you," Pat replied.

"See you later, Dan'l Boone," Matt said to Denny with a grin.

"Me, too," Pat said, and trooped out after his brother.

Denny heard the murmur of the brothers' voices as they marched along the landing, heard it briefly again but even less distinctly as they went down the stairs. Then there was silence. It was broken minutes later when Denny heard the front door open and close, heard a quick step on the stairs that he recognized as Kate's. A minute passed, then she came into the room, perched herself on the edge of the bed as she had done before, squirmed back till the bedpost stopped further movement, and settling herself comfortably, looked at Denny and said:

"You've changed. You aren't the same boy who once asked me to be his girl."

"Lot o' things have happened t'me since then, Kate, even though none o' them's had anything to do with you, or with how I feel about you. That hasn't changed."

"Things have happened to us too, Denny."

"I know."

She was silent again, but only briefly.

"You're worried about the outcome of the trial, aren't you?"

"I don't wanna go to prison."

101

"Mr. Wicker doesn't seem to think you will."

"I sure hope he's right," Denny said fervently.

"I wonder if it isn't your lack of faith in him that's responsible for the way you're worrying?"

"Nope," he said firmly. "It isn't that at all. Your Pa said this Wicker's a good lawyer, didn't he? That's good enough for me."

"Then what is it that's worrying you?"

"For one thing, Kate, that judge. What he believes and what he doesn't, and who he believes and who he thinks is lyin'. On top o' that, more than anything, I'd like to know who the witness is who says I lied about how Marv Horton got himself shot. I didn't see anybody around, and I don't think your Pa or the boys did either."

"I don't know what to say to relieve your mind, Denny. I can only tell you to believe in Mr. Wicker. You've got to. You haven't any alternative. He isn't new at this lawyer business. He's had plenty of experience. So I'm sure he'll know how to deal with the judge and with the witness too. I've got things to do, Denny. So if you don't mind . . . "

"You go ahead an' do what you have to, Kate."

"I'll be up again, as I said, right after I set the table for supper."

He smiled a little and said:

"You won't hafta go looking for me. Pretty safe bet I'll be right here."

She smiled back at him and went out.

They were in the middle of their supper, with Kate and Denny sitting on one side of the table and the boys on the other side—the chair that had been the elder Matt McEntee's was vacant and pushed in close to the table—when they heard a rap on the front door. Kate and her brothers looked at each other wonderingly. It was Pat who got up and went to the door.

"Oh," they heard Pat say in surprise after he had opened it. "Mr. Wicker! Didn't expect to see you back so soon. Come in."

"Thank you, my boy."

They heard the door close. Matt pushed his chair back from the table and got to his feet. Mark Wicker, looking a little tired, came striding into the kitchen with Pat a step or two behind him. Kate had just gotten to her feet too.

102

"Forgive me, please, for interrupting your supper," the lawyer said. "But I had to see Matt."

"You'll join us, won't you?" Kate asked, pointing to her father's chair.

"Thank you, but I had a bite to eat with Marshal Thurlow and one of his men, Bill something-or-other . . . "

"Bill Thompson," Matt said.

Wicker nodded and continued " . . . before I decided to see Matt without delay. If I may though, I'll be glad to join you when you have your coffee."

"Of course," Kate said.

Matt, moving alertly, pulled out the chair for Wicker. As the latter seated himself, Kate, Matt and Pat sat down too. Matt looked questioningly at the lawyer.

"What'd you wanna see me about?" he finally asked.

"I'd like you to tell me everything you can about a girl named Cassie Newell."

Matt stared at him.

"Cassie Newell?" he repeated. "What's she got to do with this . . . with Denny and the trial?"

"In a word, Matt, everything. Cassie Newell happens to be the one who claims to have witnessed the shooting of Marv Horton and who is prepared to take the stand and swear she heard you and your father put Denny up to killing Horton," Wicker explained. "You are to appear in court with Denny, charged with being an accessory to the crime. I posted a five hundred dollar bond for you, guaranteeing your appearance in court. So now I have two clients to defend instead of one. Now tell me about that Newell girl."

ELEVEN

A vacant store that had been pretty thoroughly aired out provided the courtroom setting for Denny's trial. Fortunately it was the largest store in Ludlow. It had to be to accommodate the numbers of townspeople who had come swarming in the moment the double doors were opened. There was not a single spectator's chair unoccupied by the time that Denny, with Marshal Thurlow at his side and Mark Wicker following them, had entered the place. A three-foot-wide aisle that began a step or two from the

103

doors led directly to the far end, where a small table that served as Judge Roland's bench had been placed. The judge was seated behind it talking with a backturned man who turned out to be the court clerk. A vacant chair that stood next to the table took the place of the witness stand. A dozen feet to the left of it and at right angles to it were two rows of three chairs each. They were already occupied by the jury of six men whose names had been drawn out of a hat. At right angles to the jury box was a second table at which Alec Murray, the country prosecutor, was seated. Murray was reading from a small sheaf of papers that he had placed before him. Just across from Murray's table on the opposite side of the aisle was still another table. Wicker with Denny on one side of him and Matt on the other side occupied it. Directly behind them sat Jake Long and Pat McEntee with Kate between them. Denny, attired in a new suit and wearing new boots, but with his head still bandaged, sat quietly and motionlessly with his gaze fixed upon the judge. He had already spotted the sheriff standing near a far side wall; he did not look at Smith a second time. Thurlow kept walking up and down the aisle, a constant reminder to the spectators that nothing that would interfere with the business at hand would be tolerated. When the court clerk moved away from the judge's table and took up his position fairly close by, Roland rapped on the table and a low murmur of talk among the onlookers died away.

"This court is now in session," the judge announced, and added: "There will be no talking among the spectators and no demonstrations of any kind. Anyone who interrupts the processes of law will be promptly ejected. Clerk, will you read the charge against the defendant?"

He held out a paper to the clerk who took it and read aloud from it. All Denny remembered of it later was, "Denny McCune, you are charged with the willful slaying of one Marv Horton. How do you plead?"

Motioning to Denny to keep his seat, Wicker arose, and with all eyes holding on him, said simply and clearly: "Not guilty," and sat down again.

Again the clerk read from the paper: "Matthew McEntee, you are charged with instigating, aiding and abetting the slaying of one Marv Horton. How do you plead?"

Wicker arose a second time and said as he had before:

104

"Not guilty," and again seated himself. The clerk returned the paper to the judge who looked at Murray and said to him:

"You may present your case, Mr. Prosecutor."

Murray, a middle-aged, average-sized man with gray-tinged brown hair, got up, came out from behind his table, and facing the jury, began with:

"Gentlemen of the jury, you have heard the charges against the two defendants. We are primarily concerned with the defendant McCune who is accused of having fired the shot or shots that took the life of the aforementioned Marv Horton. While we are also concerned with the defendant McEntee, his fate will depend upon your verdict in regard to the defendant McCune. If you find the defendant McCune guilty as charged, the court will impose the proper sentence upon McEntee. If you find McCune innocent of the charges filed against him, both defendants will be freed. Now I should like to give you the facts pertinent to the charge of murder in the first degree against the defendant McCune."

Murray then proceeded to detail the shooting of Horton. When he was finished, he said: "There was but one witness to the instigated slaying of Marv Horton, a decent, law-abiding man who was known to all of you." He turned in Smith's direction and said: "Sheriff, will you produce the witness, please?"

Smith didn't answer. He turned and walked to a small door that obviously opened into a back room, opened the door and held it wide. A girl emerged into the courtroom proper, a pretty girl who looked flushed and somewhat uneasy and who averted her eyes. Smith led her toward the judge's table only to have the clerk wave him off. The sheriff looked annoyed. He gave the clerk a hard look, turned and sauntered back to where he had been standing before. The clerk stopped the girl as she was about to seat herself in the witness' chair, took a Bible that Roland held out to him, instructed the girl to place her left hand on the Bible and to raise her right hand, and proceeded to administer the usual oath.

"Do you solemnly swear to tell the truth, the whole truth, so help you God?" he asked her.

"I do," was the low-voiced reply.

"Speak up, please," the judge said.

She half-turned to him and repeated: "I do."

"State your name," the clerk directed her.

"Cassandra Newell."

"Be seated."

The girl sat down. The clerk turned away and Murray came forward. He had a sheaf of papers in his hand that he held out to her. She took it and raised her eyes to him.

"Miss Newell, is that the affidavit that you signed of your own free will?" Murray asked her.

She glanced at the first page and looked up again.

"It is."

"Will you read it aloud, please, loud and clear so that Judge Roland and the jury will be able to hear you?"

She had a handkerchief balled up in her left hand. She dabbed at her eyes with it and, holding it ready for further use, began to read. Denny had difficulty hearing her. Apparently Roland did too, for he stopped her shortly with:

"Miss Newell, I must ask you again to raise your voice. I had to strain to hear you and I'm sure the jury did too. And since you are reading the affidavit for the jury's benefit, they must be able to hear everything. Go on, please."

The girl went on reading, a little louder this time, and Denny was able to catch something here and there. Then his thoughts wandered, and while he could hear her voice, it was as though it was coming at him from a distance. Suddenly Denny was jolted back to reality. In rising, Wicker's right arm brushed against him, and Denny looked at him.

"No, thank you. I have no desire to see the affidavit," he heard the lawyer say, and Denny saw Murray hand the papers to the judge who placed them on the table with the Bible on top of them.

Turning again to Wicker, Murray asked:

"Do you wish to examine the witness?"

"Indeed I do," Wicker replied, and Denny had to push in closer to the table in order to permit the lawyer to get past him. Wicker sauntered forward and halted a foot or so from the Newell girl, looked at her and smiled and said:

"You're a very pretty girl, Miss Newell."

"Thank you."

"I believe everyone calls you Cassie. May I take the liberty of calling you that too?"

106

"If you want to."

"Thank you. Cassie, I don't want to make this any more of an ordeal for you than is necessary. However, some of the questions I am going to put to you may awaken painful memories. So I must ask you to bear with me and remember that it is not my purpose to hurt you in any way. It is my job, my duty to my client, and I have no alternative."

She made no response. Instead she dabbed again at her eyes.

"Cassie, who helped you prepare your affidavit?"

"No one did."

"Well, who suggested the idea of the affidavit to you?"

"I don't remember."

"It couldn't have been Mr. Murray since he arrived in town only a short while ago, or so I have been told. What did Sheriff Smith have to do with it? He suggested it, didn't he, and didn't he tell you what to say in it? Before you answer, Cassie, do you now what it means to offer perjured testimony?"

"I think it means untruthful."

"I'll accept that for our purposes even though the usual definition is false testimony. Do you know that the law prescribes a penalty, usually a prison sentence, for anyone who offers false testimony?"

There was no response.

"Where did you prepare your affidavit?"

"At home."

"Then didn't your parents and the sheriff help refresh your memory, and didn't they suggest things for you to include in your affidavit?"

"They might have refreshed my memory," Cassie conceded a little uncomfortably, fussing with the skirt of her dress.

"Why the affidavit, Cassie, instead of taking the witness stand as you are doing now?"

"I thought the affidavit would be enough, and that I wouldn't have to appear here at all," she answered, flushing again. "But Judge Roland said I'd have to appear here anyway."

"I see. And why did you decide to tell your story? Because you felt it was your duty?"

"Yes. And because I wanted everyone to know the truth

107

about the McEntees and about him," and Cassie pointed to Denny who stared back at her.

"Isn't it fact though, Cassie, that your story was your way of hitting back at Matt McEntee for his failure to marry you, especially after you had confided to your family and friends that he was going to?"

"No," she replied, reddening.

"Still bearing in mind that you are testifying under oath, tell me this, please. Did Matt McEntee ever tell you right out that he was going to marry you?" Wicker pressed the girl. "Or did you assume that he was because he was seeing you often?"

Head bowed, she began to sob.

"Come, come, Cassie," the lawyer persisted. "I'm waiting for your answer. Did Matt McEntee ever propose to you? Did he ever actually mention the word marriage to you?"

"I . . . I'm not sure," she answered between sobs. "You're getting me all confused. You don't give me a chance to think."

Alec Murray arose, and when Wicker saw the judge look at the prosecutor, he too looked at Murray.

"Counsel is browbeating the witness," Murray said.

"I'm trying to get the truth from this witness," Wicker retorted.

"I fail to find anything wrong with Mr. Wicker's examination," Roland said. "You may proceed, Mr. Wicker."

"Thank you, Your Honor," the latter said, and as he turned again to Cassie, Murray sat down. "For the third time, Miss Newell, isn't it a fact that Matt McEntee never proposed to you and that he never spoke of marriage to you?"

Again the girl began to sob.

"I . . . I think he did," she faltered.

"Did what?" Wicker thundered at her. "The truth, Cassie Newell! The truth!"

Tears were coursing down her cheeks, streaking them.

"I don't remember now for sure," she said, dabbing at her eyes. "But we were seeing so much of each other, he must have one time or another."

"Were you in love with him?"

She didn't voice her answer; she nodded.

"Do you think he was in love with you?"

"I . . . I thought he was," was the faltering reply.

"If he didn't say so in many words, did he act like a man who was in love?"

Again she nodded.

"But then for some reason known only to you, you fell out of love with him. And when that happened you sought only one thing, to hurt him as much as you could regardless of the consequences to either of you. And if you had to lie to destroy him, you were willing. Isn't that true, Miss Newell?"

Her head came down and she sobbed anew. The lawyer frowned, turned and looked at the judge. The latter leaned over the table.

"Miss Newell, would you like a few minutes' time in which to compose yourself?"

"Yes, please."

"You may stand down."

She got to her feet, and as she fled across the courtroom, all eyes followed her. Smith opened the door to the back room; she flashed past him and he closed the door behind her and slowly returned to his original post.

"I reserve the right to continue my examination of Miss Newell when she is ready to continue," Wicker said, addressing the judge.

"Yes, Mr. Wicker," Roland acknowledged, and as the lawyer turned and retraced his steps to his table, the judge said: "You may call your next witness, Mr. Murray."

"Thank you, sir," the prosecutor responded. "I call Sheriff Smith to the stand."

Everyone's eyes focused on the sheriff. He looked surprised and flustered, evidence that he had not expected to be called upon to testify, and further, that he did not like the idea. However, there was nothing he could do about it. So he tried to square his rounded, sagging shoulders and marched across the room only to be halted near the judge's table by the clerk, Bible in hand. Smith was quickly sworn and seated. Murray sauntered forward.

"How long have you been sheriff of this community?" he asked.

"Oh, four months, give or take a day or so."

"Sheriff, in your position, I would assume that you must

109

know everyone in your community and probably all there is to know about everyone."

" 'Course."

"What was the general opinion among your townspeople of the late McEntee?"

"Folks around Ludlow didn't like him. Feeling's just about the same for his son," Smith answered, pointed to Matt and said: "That one. The other son's no bargain either, far's that goes."

"Did you ever have any trouble with the McEntees?" Murray asked the sheriff.

"With the father. I handled the sons without 'ny trouble."

"Do you recall any one specific instance . . . ?"

"When I hadda get after the father?"

"Yes."

"No, not offhand. It was just that McEntee thought he could walk all over anybody who got in his way. I hadda call him on that a couple o' times just so he'd know there was somebody around who wasn't ascared o' him."

"This one last question, Sheriff. Did you have anything at all to do with Miss Newell's affidavit?"

"Nope. Not a blamed thing."

"Thank you, Sheriff. Mr. Wicker . . . ?"

The lawyer arose and came forward. Smith looked uneasy. He kept pushing his spectacles up on his nose.

"Were you elected or appointed to your job?"

"Town council appointed me."

"The members of the council were friends of yours, weren't they?"

"Against the law for a man to have friends?" Smith countered.

"Answer the question, Sheriff," Judge Roland said curtly.

"Yes, sir," Smith said rather grumpily. Then to Wicker: "Yeah, they were friends o' mine and still are. What about it?"

Wicker smiled and said:

"Just this much about it, Sheriff. I have spoken to the town councilmen. Two of the three members have never considered themselves friends of yours, while the third one begged the question. In addition, two of them were not par-

110

ticularly impressed by your performance in office while the third one again declined to voice an opinion. Finally, they didn't come to you and ask you to take the job. They tell me, and the third one was included in this, you solicited the job. Since there were signs of impending trouble here, there were no other applicants for the job, and since the town needed someone in the sheriff's office, they gave you the job even though they weren't overly enthused about pinning the star on you. What was your occupation before you were made sheriff?"

"Storekeeper."

"Were you successful in that undertaking?"

"I did all right for myself."

Wicker flashed him an odd smile, dug in his pocket and produced a couple of folded sheets of paper that he unfolded as he looked up.

"I have here a statement from your bank, Sheriff, the Bank of Ludlow. It shows that over the past five years you borrowed more than sixteen hundred dollars from the bank in three separate loans. To date, that is as of yesterday, you have repaid exactly one hundred dollars plus the interest on the sixteen hundred. Your storekeeping was so successful that you still owe your suppliers a total of two thousand eight dollars and sixteen cents. The attorneys for two of your former suppliers have already contacted the town council in an effort to have your wages turned over to them to be applied to your indebtedness to their clients. They have threatened to take legal action against the council unless their request is honored and complied with."

Smith offered no comment. He looked hard at Wicker, but wisely held his tongue. The lawyer pocketed his papers, smiled again at the sheriff and began again, this time with:

"Sheriff, when the prosecutor asked you if you had had anything whatsoever to do with Miss Newell's affidavit, you insisted you hadn't. But isn't it a fact, Sheriff, that the idea originated with you and that it was at your instance that the Newells, Cassie's mother and father, hounded her into preparing it and then inserted things in it that she hadn't witnessed and which were entirely figments of your imagination? If you deny that, Sheriff, I'll insist that the court hold you for perjury and deal with you in accordance with the law."

111

"Just a moment, please, Mr. Wicker," Judge Roland said. "Sheriff . . ."

The latter, redfaced, turned slowly toward the judge.

"Sheriff," Roland said. "I want you to tell me if what Mr. Wicker claims is true or false. Remember, you are still under oath. Now answer me."

Smith moistened his lips with his tongue. He gulped and swallowed hard.

"Yeah," he conceded, averting his eyes. "It's true. Only I felt I had to do it. I was afraid if I didn't, the McEntees would get bolder an' bolder steppin' on folks and that others would follow their lead and pretty soon nobody'd have 'ny respect for the law or for me."

"Take off that star," the judge ordered him, and held out his hand for it. Smith unpinned it, held it in his hand and looked hard and unhappily at it, sighed and passed it to Roland, who put it on the table in front of him, looked up and called out: "Marshal Thurlow."

The latter had been standing near the open doors. He came striding down the aisle.

"Yes, sir?"

"Marshal, take this man," the judge directed, and pointed to Smith, "into custody until I decide what to do with him."

"Right, Judge," Thurlow said. "Let's go, Smith."

The unhappy man got up slowly, heavily too. Thurlow took him by the arm and led him up the aisle and out of the courtroom. A barely audible buzz of whispering ranged about through the spectators. But Roland ignored it.

"Mr. Wicker," he said and the whispering died out, "I am prepared to entertain a motion for dismissal of the charges against both of your clients."

"Thank you, sir," Wicker said. "But before I offer such a motion, may I approach the bench?"

"Of course."

Wicker turned and beckoned to Murray who arose and came forward and followed him to the judge's table, and the two men bent over it. However, it was Wicker who did the talking. When he finished, both Roland and Murray nodded. The latter turned and went back to his seat while Wicker stepped back.

"Matt McEntee to the stand, please," the judge said, and

Matt got up and came out from behind the table. "Clerk," Roland added, "please bring Miss Newell out here and seat her at Mr. Wicker's table. Then you may swear Mr. McEntee."

Cassie looked apprehensively at Wicker when she emerged from the back room. When she saw Matt waiting to be sworn, she flushed and hastily averted her eyes. When she was led to Wicker's table, she looked puzzled. She flushed again when she met Kate's eyes and hastily seated herself as the clerk directed, in Matt's chair. The oath was administered to Matt and the youth sat down and looked up as Wicker approached. The lawyer smiled at him reassuringly.

"Matt," he began. "Will you tell the court, please, about your relationship with Cassie Newell?"

Matt nodded and said:

"Yeah, sure, Mr. Wicker. Only where d'you want me to begin? Like I told you, I went to the same school she did only I was a couple o' grades higher'n she was because I was older."

"Yes, and you also told me how much you liked her."

"That's right," Matt acknowledged, and with something of a wistful smile added: "I still do."

He squirmed back in his chair, settling himself a little more comfortably.

"I didn't see Cassie for quite a spell after I got out school," he heard Matt say, and Denny stole a quick look at the Newell girl who was sitting just a few feet away from him. She was a pretty girl, he agreed. But Kate was just as pretty, perhaps even prettier. He decided he liked Kate's kind better. He admitted he was prejudiced, but quickly added that he had a right to be. Kate would never do to any man what Cassie had done to Matt. He turned his head again in Matt's direction when he heard him say: "I was too busy learning my father's business. Then one day when I had to go into town, I ran into her. She'd gotten even prettier than the last time I'd seen her. We got to talking and I wound up asking her to go driving with me. She accepted and that's how it began."

Matt paused briefly, then he went on again.

"Guess I must've taken Cassie driving, oh, seven or eight, maybe even nine times besides takin' her to a barn

113

dance over to Stafford, and then over to Eagle Pass to a party that the Gibsons, friends o' my father's, threw for one o' their daughters. We had a good time both times. We got along just fine, Cassie an' me. Guess I liked her a heap better'n any girl I'd ever known."

"Think you might have wound up marrying her?" Wicker asked.

"Yes, I think I would've," Matt replied. "Fact is, Mr. Wicker, I'm pretty sure I would've. Only when I figgered I was ready, though, and not when somebody else thought I oughta."

"You were pretty close to your father, I understand. Did you ever discuss Cassie with him?"

"Yeah, sure."

"Did you discuss with him the possibility that you might marry her?"

"Uh-huh."

"What was his reaction?"

"Oh, Pop was all for it. Y'see, he knew Cassie and he liked her. Only he wasn't what you might call taken with her folks. So he thought I oughta wait a bit longer, go on seeing Cassie and see how things worked out before I made my move. I think he wanted to see how I'd be getting along with her folks before I decided to get married."

"What caused the break with Cassie?"

"Way I remember it, it was right after I'd talked with Pop. I'd picked Cassie up in front o' her house and headed outta town. It was a beautiful night and the countryside never smelled better. It was like driving through a big garden. I noticed that Cassie was awf'lly quiet and that wasn't her way with me, ever. We'd always had so much to talk about before that. I kept asking her to tell me what was troubling her. She cried a little and said she shouldn't have come with me, that she should have stayed at home, and asked me to take her back. I pulled up, turned her around to me and made her tell me what was up. Seems her mother'd begun hounding her. She'd told Cassie she had to pin me down. Either we were gonna set a date right then for us to get married or Cassie wasn't to see me again. Guess I got my back up. I don't like bein' crowded into doing anything. I wanna do the deciding for myself and I don't aim to let anybody else force my hand. So I turned

114

the rig around and took Cassie home. I never saw her again after that."

Denny stole another look at Cassie. Her head was down and she was sobbing, quietly though, so that no one other than Denny was aware of it.

"Matt, do you think she would have done anything to hurt you? That is, of her own free will?" Wicker asked.

"No, sir," Matt answered firmly. "There's no meanness in her."

"Then you think that she was, we-ll, driven to do what she did?"

Matt nodded and said:

"I'm willing to bet on it."

"How do you feel about her now?"

"Same's I did before."

"Any animosity?"

"No, sir."

Wicker turned to Judge Roland and nodded, and the latter said:

"You may step down, Mr. McEntee."

"Yes, sir," Matt answered.

"Take my seat at the table," Wicker told him.

"Right."

As Matt started back to the table, Wicker addressed the judge.

"Your honor, I now move for the dismissal of the charges against my clients."

Roland nodded and said:

"The charges are dismissed and the defendants released, and their bonds returned to them."

"Thank you, sir. In my clients' behalf, I ask that no charges be brought against either Miss Newell or Sheriff Smith. Miss Newell has amply indicated her desire to make amends with her tears. As for the sheriff, removal from office should be sufficient punishment for him."

"Very well, Mr. Wicker. This court is willing to accept your clients' recommendation. No charges will be brought against Miss Newell or Sheriff Smith." Roland turned to the jury. "Thank you, gentlemen, for your close attention to the business before us. You are dismissed." Then facing the spectators, the judge announced: "This court stands adjourned."

TWELVE

As Mark Wicker neared the defense counsel's table he saw that Cassie Newell was still occupying Matt's chair while the latter was sitting in his, Wicker's, place with Denny on Matt's right.

"Come on, son," he said to Denny.

Denny got up at once. Wicker motioned to Kate, Pat and Jake Long and the three of them arose together, fell in behind Denny, who was following Wicker, and marched up the aisle to the open door. Thurlow, who was standing there, stopped the lawyer and said to him:

"That man an' woman I was just talkin' to, they're the girl's folks."

"Oh?"

"I told them there wasn't any point in them hangin' around here 'less they were lookin' for trouble, that if somebody was to tell the judge who they are, he might decide to call them back and give them a good layin' out for what they talked their girl into doing."

"I'm surprised he didn't have them brought in," Wicker confided. "If he had, I don't think he would have spared them any. However, since he didn't . . ."

He shrugged and stepped outside. Thurlow patted Denny on the back.

"Glad you made out the way you did, boy," he said.

Denny smiled at him and answered: "Thanks, Marshal. I'm glad too."

They gathered around Wicker on the walk. The spectators, they noticed, who had trooped out earlier were walking off in different directions.

"I'm obliged to you, Mr. Wicker," Denny said to the lawyer, "for gettin' me outta that fix. Guess you must be just about the best lawyer anywhere."

"We-ll, not quite, Denny," Wicker responded with a light laugh. "But it's good of you to say that."

"We're all indebted to you, Mr. Wicker," Kate told him. "And we'll never forget it."

"You may think otherwise when you get my bill."

"No," Kate assured him with a shake of her head. "We won't."

"Wonder how long Matt figures to be?" Pat asked.

"Why don't you people wait for him in your rig?" Wicker suggested. "Lots more comfortable sitting than standing around, you know."

Pat turned to Kate and asked:

"Think maybe I oughta go back inside and see what's keepin' him?"

Before Kate could answer, Wicker said:

"I wouldn't if I were you," and added with a little smile: "You might find yourself interrupting something and I know you wouldn't want to do that."

"Gotta remember that like they say," Jake Long put in with a grin, "two's company an' three's a crowd."

"Yeah?" Pat retorted. "What about the judge? He's still in there, isn't he?"

"Yes," Wicker said. "But he's probably so occupied writing his report of the trial that he isn't even aware of their presence."

"I'm hungry," Pat said a little grumpily.

"Can't you wait till we get home?" Kate asked him. "If you must have something now, go over to the hotel, get yourself something to eat there and follow us home."

"I c'n wait," Pat answered.

Thurlow had closed the door to the courtroom and was standing squarely in front of it. Suddenly it was opened from the inside. The marshal turned quickly. When he saw that it was Matt, he nodded and stepped aside so that the youth could pass him. All eyes held on Matt as he came across the walk. He was grave-faced.

"Let's go home," he said simply.

" 'Bout time," Pat said.

Ignoring him, Matt turned to Wicker.

"Pop was supposed to know more about cattle than anybody around," he told the lawyer. "Kinda think he was smarter'n most too when it came to pickin' himself a lawyer. You did a fine job for us, Mr. Wicker, and we sure appreciate it."

"Thank you, Matt," Wicker replied. "I'm glad I was able to be of service to you."

The two shook hands.

117

"Soon's you get your bill to me," Matt said, "I'll have the bank pay it."

The lawyer nodded and turned after them as Matt led them to their waiting rig. At Jake Long's instance, Denny climbed up first. Then Jake turned and helped Kate mount the high step. Denny reached down and gave her a steadying hand and a moment later she was sitting beside him. Long stepped down into the gutter, came around the rig to the other side of it and hoisted himself up. As he unwound the reins from around the handbrake, he turned his head and looked at Matt and Pat who had already untied their horses and mounted them.

The rig wheeled around, and with the McEntee boys riding close behind it, rumbled away. The street wasn't quite as thronged as it had been earlier. Obviously many of the townspeople who had turned out for the trial had already returned to their homes. But those who were still about stopped and lifted their gaze to the McEntee party as it came abreast of them and followed it with their eyes as it passed them and headed downstreet and took the westward road.

There was little conversation aboard the rig. It consisted of the following between Kate and Denny. Turning and looking at him, Kate asked:

"Feel all right?"

"Yeah, sure."

"Head ache?"

"No. Fact is, I feel pretty good right now. Specially now that that court business is outta the way."

"Just the same, after you've had something to eat, I think you ought to go upstairs and rest a while."

"Y'mean get into bed?"

"No. Change your clothes and make yourself comfortable in that big chair in my father's room."

"Something else I wanted to talk to you about. Your Ma did a pretty good job o' teaching you, didn't she?"

"I think she did. Why? Why do you ask?"

"I never got much schoolin'. Most o' what I know I got from my Pa. I don't wanna start schoolin' now. I'd find myself in a class with a lot o' kids a lot younger'n me, and I wouldn't like that. Besides, goin' to school wouldn't leave me much time to do what I wanna do around here, do something to earn my keep. Think you could do for me what your Ma did for you? I'd try awf'lly hard to learn from you. What d'you think?"

She smiled at him and said:

"All right, Denny. As long as you're willing, I am, too."

"Swell, Kate. And thanks."

But Denny's instruction did not begin right away. In fact it was delayed for several days due to his insistence that he be given an opportunity to help the boys and the crew resume the McE's business. There were so many long unfilled orders for cattle that it became quite hectic cutting out and bunching together the number of head needed to fill the individual orders and then keeping them separated until the twenty-two mile drive to the railroad was begun. Denny was permitted to lend a hand here and there, but Matt refused to let him overdo. He turned down Denny's request to be allowed to take a hand in the drive so bluntly that the boy was almost crushed.

"Now look," Matt told him, taking him aside. "You're just beginning to look and feel like yourself. Finish that job and finish it right before you go takin' on anything more. Givin' us a hand gettin' the stock ready for shipping out was fine. Now that that's over an' done with, you hustle yourself back to the house an' get together with Kate. I wanna hear good things about you from her. When she's finished with you, you're gonna be turned over to Jake Long so's he c'n start teaching you the cattle business so that when the time comes for you to take your place alongside o' Pat an' me you'll be ready and able. We've got a good business to run and it's gonna get bigger and you're gonna be needed. You've got a stake in the McE same's we have and you're gonna be expected to do your share of what has to be done to keep the McE on top. Now g'wan. Back to the house with you and tell Kate you're reporting for schoolwork duty."

It was two days later. Save for one man, Lee Dibbs, who had been left behind with instructions to keep an eye on things, and that included riding out a couple of times a day to check on the small bunch of steers that remained unsold out of the huge herd, the McE appeared to be deserted. It

119

would be at least three days, and in all probability four, Matt had estimated, before he, Pat, Jake and the rest of the crew returned. Denny was upstairs, sitting at the window in the late Matt McEntee's room, in the big easy chair that had been the dead man's. One of Kate's books, a grammar, was open in his lap. Squaring back in the chair for a moment's resting of his eyes, he happened to look out toward the road that led to town. He rubbed his eyes and looked a second time when he spotted two mounted men idling in the gateway, looking around them interestedly, and then focusing their gaze on the house. He wondered about them, wondered who they were and what they were doing there, and watched them intently, wishing the while that he could see their faces more clearly. When he saw them knee-nudge their horses into movement and saw them coming toward the barn with one man giving more than a passing glance at the bunkhouse, Denny closed the book, left it on the armrest, and got up. When the two walked their horses past the barn, he was able to get a better look at them. He went racing out of the room, dashed down the landing to his own room; a minute later he reappeared on the landing, clutching the old buffalo gun in his left hand. He scurried down the stairs, whirled around and panted into the kitchen. Ming, who was putting some dishes in the cupboard above the iron sink, and Kate, who was bending over and folding some towels on the table, looked around at him.

"You shouldn't rush around like that," she said. "You aren't up to that yet." Apparently she hadn't noticed that he was carrying his gun. But then she did, and she looked troubled. "What's . . . what's that for?"

"Two men comin' toward the house," he told her, still breathing hard. "Don't think I ever saw th'm before. What's more, I don't like their looks." She straightened up and came around the table. "You'll have to answer the door, Kate, when they come up to it and knock. Only you won't open it. You'll ask who they are and what they want, and no matter what they tell you, you'll tell them to come back some other time. Get it?"

"Yes," she replied. "But I don't like it."

"That makes two of us."

She paled when they heard heavy, scuffing bootsteps on the veranda.

120

"There they are," Denny said. "Now look. I'll be near the stairs. When I tell you to get away from the door, move an' move fast, and as far outta the way as you c'n get. Be even better if you turn tail and run back in here." There was a heavy-handed knock on the door. "C'mon."

He followed her out of the kitchen, backed against the lowest step of the stairway and half-raised his gun. Kate glanced around at him; when he nodded, she turned, and facing the door, asked a little quiveringly:

"Yes?"

"Howdy, Ma'am. We'd like to talk to the boss if he's around."

Denny knew he had never heard the voice before. Instinctively his curled finger tightened around the buffalo gun's trigger.

"He isn't here," he heard Kate answer.

"Oh? Then how about us talkin' to you, Ma'am? Be better though if you'd open the door a mite. Don't like talkin' through a closed door. Nothing to be a-scared of, y'know. How about it?"

Kate shot a look over her shoulder at Denny. When he shook his head, she said, a little steadier-voiced than before:

"You'll have to come back another time."

With that she stepped back from the door and shot another look at Denny who hissed at her:

"The kitchen."

She needed no urging. She fled through the portiered doorway.

"Ma'am?" the man asked. "You still there?"

Denny raised his gun a little higher. The doorknob turned as Denny expected it to. The door itself was opened the barest bit, then a little wider and even wider. The worn, scuffed, booted foot of a man appeared astride the doorway strip to prevent the door's being slammed on him. Then a battered hat and the unshaven face of the man were poked in. He stole a quick look behind the door. When he failed to see anyone there, he opened the door wider. He was about average sized. The clothes he was wearing were a couple of sizes too big for him. They must have been discarded by their original owner, Denny decided, and left in the latter's barn and stolen from there.

121

"All right, Shorty," the man said low-voiced over his shoulder to a companion whom Denny couldn't see. "C'mon."

Denny had glided away from the stairs and had backed against the stairway wall. Standing there motionlessly in the shadows that played over it, he had, not surprisingly, not been noticed. The first man stepped inside. The man whom he had called Shorty crowded in behind, then moved up alongside of him.

"What d'we do now, Mike?" he asked in a guarded voice.

Mike was looking in the direction of the kitchen as though he were wondering with overwhelming curiosity what lay on the other side of the portiere.

"You go upstairs an' look around," he instructed Shorty, "while I go have a look in there," and he indicated the kitchen with a nod.

"Don't move, either one o' you," Denny commanded, and the two men stared at him. "Or I'll blow you two buzzards to bits."

Shorty gulped and swallowed abruptly. Mike turned hard, narrowed eyes upon Denny.

"Where'd you come from, boy?" he asked.

"Go easy with him, Mike," Shorty said, side-mouthed, to his slightly taller companion. "I don't like the looks o' that shotgun."

"He's only a sprout an' sprouts don't scare me none," Mike retorted.

"This one's different," Denny said evenly. "This one knows how to shoot and isn't afraid to. You, Mike, with your left hand, and careful-like too if you wanna stay alive an' all in one piece, unbuckle your gunbelt and let it drop."

"Suppose you make me do it," Mike said tauntingly.

"If I hafta, I will," Denny answered. He lowered the buffalo gun the barest bit so that its fire-blackened, gaping muzzle held on a line with the buckle on Mike's pants belt. "Case you don't know what a buffalo gun c'n do to a man, I'll tell you. It makes one heckuva hole in him. Now 'less you wanna see what your guts look like when they spill outta you . . . "

"Better do like he says, Mike," Shorty said. "Sprout or no, I kinda think . . . "

122

"Nobody asked you," Mike flung back at him.

Someone came gliding in from the veranda with a half-raised rifle holding on Mike. It was Kate and she prodded him in the back with the muzzle.

"I think you'd better do as you're told," she said quietly.

Mike scowled darkly. He was motionless till he was jabbed a second time, and this time Kate was anything but gentle about it. He unbuckled his gunbelt with his left hand and let it fall. The holstered gun lay half on his left boot toe and half off.

"Kick it over here," Denny ordered.

Mike's eyes gleamed. He didn't kick the gun very hard, only hard enough to spin it around so that it came to a stop about midway between Denny and himself.

"Your turn, Shorty," Denny said.

The man winced when Kate poked him in the small of the back.

"Haven't got a gun on me," he said. "Only this," and he pointed to the handle of a knife that was sticking out of the top of his boot.

"Slide it over the floor," Denny told him. "Kate, hold your gun on his loud-mouthed partner. If he makes the tiniest move, put a slug in him."

Mike's eyes burned at him. But Denny ignored it. Shorty bent over and eased the knife out of his boot. He stole a guarded upward look at Denny; when the buffalo gun moved and held on him and the muzzle seemed to yawn hungrily at him, he gulped and losing his nerve, slid his knife over the floor in Denny's direction. It struck Mike's gun and caromed off, spun around for a moment and lay still. It was then that Mike chose to make his move.

"Jump her!" he yelled to Shorty, and dove at Denny with his arms outflung, coming in low at him in an effort to avoid being shot if Denny fired.

Alertly, Denny side-stepped, and half-turning, drove the heavy butt of his gun squarely at Mike's head. Solidly hit, Mike was stunned. He fell face downward on the floor with his arms still outflung. Shorty was on the floor too. But he was sitting on it, holding his head with both hands, rocking from side to side, and moaning:

"Oh, my head, my head! You busted it open!"

Looking at Denny, Kate said:

"I thought he was going to turn on me. So I hit him."

"You did right," Denny told her.

The thump of approaching horses' hoofs carried to the house. Kate turned and stole a quick look through the open door. Circling around the motionless Mike, Denny peered out too. Three mounted men came into view, loped past the barn and drummed on toward the house. Denny thought that one of them looked familiar.

"It's the marshal!" Kate said excitedly. "Marshal Thurlow!"

She backed out of the doorway, turned and waited on the veranda to meet the oncoming horsemen. Spotting the rifle in her hands, and interpreting that to mean trouble, they quickened their horses' pace. Moments later they pulled up alongside of Mike's and Shorty's horses, flung themselves off, and drawing their guns, came bounding up the steps to the veranda.

"I was never so glad to see anyone as I am to see you, Marshal," Denny heard her say to Thurlow.

The two men with him wore the same kind of badge as he did. They followed him into the house. Thurlow shot a quick look at Denny, obviously to see that he was all right. Then he glanced at Shorty, who was holding his head and still moaning although he had stopped his rocking, third, he looked down at the outsprawled figure of Mike. His companions bent over the latter and dragged him over on his back.

"Think these two are the ones we're lookin' for, Tom?" one of them asked Thurlow.

He turned and stood over Shorty, nudged him with his boottoe, and asked him:

"You, what's your name?"

"Brown," was the reply.

"And your sidekick's?"

"Watts."

"They're the ones, all right," Thurlow announced to the other two lawmen. "Those were the names I got, Brown an' Watts. Get him up on his feet," he added, pointing to Mike, "and take him outta here."

There was a general holstering of guns. Then the two marshals hauled Mike up from the floor, and half leading

124

and half dragging him, took him out of the house and down the veranda steps. One of them returned a minute or so later, bent over Shorty and got him up on his feet and led him out to join his companion.

"Got word early this morning from Crockett that two characters had busted outta the jail there," Thurlow said, first to Kate, then to Denny. "So we started ridin' around lookin' for th'm, being that they were supposed to be heading this way. Every place we came to, we stopped to warn the people to keep an eye out for those two. They give you a hard time?"

"Not too bad," Denny replied.

"I'm glad o' that," Thurlow said. He hitched up his gun-belt and shifted his holster a bit. "We-ll, gotta get moving. Bye."

"Bye, Marshal," Kate and Denny said together, and followed him out to the veranda.

Shorty had already been boosted up on his horse's back. With Thurlow lending a hand, Mike was lifted into the saddle. He sagged forward against his horse's neck. One of Thurlow's men produced a rope and Mike was lashed on. stood motionlessly and silent while he closed the door. The three lawmen climbed up on their horses. Thurlow gave Kate and Denny a half-salute as he wheeled away. With one of the other marshals leading Mike's horse and the third man riding alongside of Shorty, who seemed to have recovered from the thump on his head, the little party jogged past the barn, and after a bit, passed through the archway and wheeled toward town. When Kate turned and reentered the house, Denny followed her. She waited and Then she said:

"You could have killed those two men quite easily, couldn't you?"

"Yeah, guess I coulda."

"But you didn't. You didn't even shoot when you had the right to, when that man Mike leaped at you and you had every right to defend yourself. Why didn't you, Denny? I'm curious to know."

His shoulders lifted in an empty shrug.

"Mean you don't know?" she asked.

"Nope."

125

"Any other time you would have fired and without the least bit of hesitation."

"I know. But why I didn't this time . . . "

"Well, whatever it was that stayed your hand, I think it's a good sign. A sign that you aren't a . . . a killer as I once accused you of being. And I'm glad, Denny. Awf'lly glad."

He smiled at her although he offered no comment.

"I think you're going to turn out just fine, Denny McCune. You're going to grow into a good man."

"Thank you, Ma'am," he said gravely, despite a little grin that wrinkled the corners of his eyes and mouth.

"I mean that, Denny."

"Yes'm, I know you do. And I sure hope you're right."

"Feel up to going back to your books?"

"Yeah, sure. Only before I go back to th'm, there's something I'd like to ask you. I know you hate guns an' killing. But how come all uva sudden you forgot that and came tiptoein' in here with that rifle in your hands? And lookin' at you, and judgin' by the expression on your face, I got the feeling that if you had had to, you'da used that rifle."

"Yes, I think I would have. When I ran back into the kitchen, all I could think of was that you would be facing those two men all by yourself, and that I had deserted you. Before I realized what I was doing, I had taken a rifle from the rack in the kitchen and found myself racing around the veranda to the front door."

"Heard you tell the marshal how glad you were to see him. Wanna know something, Kate? I was doggoned glad to see you."

She flashed him a smile, turned and headed for the kitchen. He followed her with his eyes. As she neared the doorway, a head was poked out at her, a head with a black skullcap on it. It was Ming's. When Kate brushed the portiere aside, Denny saw that the Chinaman had an upraised meat cleaver in his hand. Denny grinned, picked up Mike's gunbelt and Shorty's knife and carried them upstairs with him.

It was three days later when the McEntees and their crew returned. Kate and Denny were sitting at the kitchen table having a mid-afternoon cup of coffee when the front door was flung open and Matt came striding in. He scaled his hat across the room and looked first at Kate, then at Denny.

"You two all right?" he asked.

"Of course we're all right," Kate answered.

"We came through town on our way back," Matt related. "Ran into Thurlow and he told us about those two buzzards who busted in here. Musta given you quite a scare, huh?"

"Yes, but we came out've it all right," Kate said.

"That's the last time I take the whole crew. Next time I'll see to it that Jake leaves a couple o' hands around." Matt pulled out a chair and sank down in it. "Got something I wanna talk to you about," he said to his sister.

Denny reached for his coffee cup as he started to get up. Matt looked at him and asked:

"Where are you goin'?"

"You said you wanted to talk to Kate about something. So I took that to mean it was something private."

"Sit down," Matt said, waving him down into his chair. "You aren't a stranger. You're family." When Denny had again seated himself, Matt turned again to Kate. "We came past Cassie's house and she was up at her window. She looked so doggoned low, like she'd been crying. Her mother must be makin' life miserable for her, the poor kid. It hurt me to see her lookin' like that. I love that girl, Kate, and regardless of what she let herself get talked into doing to me, I wanna marry her, and quick too."

"Then marry her."

"I aim to. Only how are you gonna feel about having her live here too? That's the only part of it that's bothering me."

"This is home to all of us, Matt," Kate said quietly. "And when you marry and Pat marries, I expect your wives to come to live here too. I don't expect either of you to move out and go somewhere else to live just because I'm here. We'll get along."

"Thanks, Kate," he said. He leaned toward her and kissed her cheek.

"How about me?" Denny asked. "Don't I get kissed too?

127

Remember, I'm family, and I don't wanna be left outta things."

"You won't be," Matt told him as he got up, rounded the table and picked up his hat. "I'll let you kiss the bride."

He clapped on his hat and went striding out of the room. Moments later they heard the front door slam behind him.